CURSE

ANU KAY

An imprint of
Srishti Publishers & Distributors

Srishti Publishers & Distributors
A unit of AJR Publishing LLP
212A, Peacock Lane
Shahpur Jat, New Delhi – 110 049
editorial@srishtipublishers.com

First Published by Launchpad,
an imprint of Srishti Publishers & Distributors in 2025

Copyright © Anu Kay, 2025

10 9 8 7 6 5 4 3 2 1

This is a work of fiction. The characters, places, organisations and events described in this book are either a work of the author's imagination or have been used fictitiously. Any resemblance to people, living or dead, places, events, communities or organisations is purely coincidental.

The author asserts the moral right to be identified as the author of this work. All rights reserved. No part of this publication may be reproduced, stored in a retrieval system, or transmitted, in any form or by any means, electronic, mechanical, photocopying, recording or otherwise, without the prior written permission of the Publishers.

Printed and bound in India

To Oliver, my rock in turbulent seas.

The Flying Peacock.

Author's Note

Lanka, the name mentioned in the Ramayana, is believed by scholars to refer to modern-day Sri Lanka, although there is no definitive proof to support this claim. In this book, Sri Lanka is also referred to as Lanka to maintain the enchantment of the epic *Ramayana*.

It's important to emphasize that while this book is a work of fiction, certain real names have been incorporated for narrative purposes. However, the storyline itself is entirely fictional.

Prologue

Lanka, Circa 1500 BCE

With a sari draped around her, fresh flowers in her silver hair, and red kumkum on her forehead, she came walking towards the backyard with her cane, producing a familiar tapping sound. Her garden was full of paraphernalia that she had collected from her ancestors. She sat with the people from her neighbourhood in a circle around the campfire to tell stories and express their fears, beliefs, and heroism. They called her Kathika, the storyteller. No one knew her real name.

"How old are you, Kathika?" a woman asked.

"I am so old that I cannot count anymore," she said. "No one I knew as a little girl is alive today. Looking back, I think of the house that was once home. Today, it looks different. The dead have a voice. They talk to me. They give me hope. The memories of all those who meant something in my life have stayed with me, just like when the sun goes down, the afterglow would remain on the surrounding hills. Today, I wish to tell you the story of our people—yours and my story."

Kathika was an enthusiastic speaker. Her narratives brought people together, creating a bond with her audience. She began to hum a song, a familiar tune, like a prayer.

Then she continued her narration: "My grandmother told me legends. I want to retell them and connect you to our past. When you understand where we came from, you'll better grasp the present and shape your future." Kathika paused, adjusted her sari, and added, "Have you heard of the mighty Asuras?"

"Yes," came the answer in one voice.

"Enlighten me, who exactly are the Asuras?"

"We are the Asuras," a man responded.

"And who is the most renowned of all Asuras?"

"Ravana, the great," a woman replied.

"I'm the descendant of Ravana," declared Kathika.

"But you don't resemble a queen," came the sceptical remark.

"No queen is a queen without her kingdom. Once upon a time, the Asuras ruled over Lanka, a kingdom that spanned the vast expanse of the Indian Ocean, extending its dominion to the Deccan plateau. The mighty Ravana ruled Lanka, a land of remarkable splendour. Among his many remarkable possessions was a wondrous flying ship." Her storytelling skill was bestowed upon her by her father and grandmother.

"A flying ship?" a man inquired.

"Yes, a flying ship," came the reply.

"I have never heard of such a thing," the man whispered.

"Follow me. I'll show it to you," the old woman said, gesturing as she led them towards a corner of the garden. Nearby, a hut stood tall and majestic, its sturdy stone walls complemented by a thatched roof that added rustic charm. Anticipation grew as they approached a grand hangar, its doors swinging open to reveal a remarkable sight. Inside, an extraordinary ship gleamed under the moonlight, its surface illuminated by rays piercing through the veil of the night sky. "Look at this, decorated with precious stones. Isn't it stunning? And inside, it has wide chambers. Isn't it marvellous?"

"I have lived in your neighbourhood all my life, and I did not know you had a ship that could fly," one of them confessed.

The flying machine measured twenty-four Hastas in

circumference and had four wheels. Hastas, an ancient unit of measurement, is approximately eighty-three centimetres. Every eye was fixed on the wondrous sight before them.

"Kathika, do you know how to fly this ship?" someone asked her.

"No, I don't, but my grandfather knew how to. I used to fly with him when I was a little girl. Oh! It is wonderful to fly. It is a great marvel. It flies swiftly in the chosen direction. It can dash through the air, sink, and rise in its fleetness, leaving behind the fury of the rushing wind, obeying the driver's will, and roaring as loud as thunder, labouring through the clouds.

"I have flown with my grandfather across the ocean into the blue sky and white clouds. I have seen the rocky shore and the forest from above, the spacious altars of the holy hermit and the green plantation where the betel grows on bent limbs. I have seen fig trees with mighty branches bowing towards the earth. The delightful scene of sandalwood trees and tall aloe trees in the grove, I enjoyed the view of the silvery streams in the forest that ran calm with fresh waters."

The old woman illustrated her memories through physical movements and expressive hand gestures. Her words transported them to a distant past, delving into the lesser-known achievements of her ancestors. With a final closure of the hangar doors and a secure lock, she led the way back to the campfire.

"This was the only flying ship that existed during the time of Ravana," she continued. "No one had seen another flying ship around Lanka. My ancestor, the one and only Ravana. Oh! I am so proud of him. He was a powerful man, great and mighty, terrible like a lion, strong, swift, and unmatched in might.

"He was a maestro of the Veena. Have you heard about the Veena? The musical instrument? He was a great scholar and author of several books. This flying ship was Ravana's favourite;

he named it Dandu Monara, which means 'The Flying Peacock' in the Sinhala language."

"Did Ravana fly the ship himself?"

"Yes, he did. They say he knew how to fly this incredible ship. When Ravana wasn't at the wheel, his guards maintained constant vigilance over it day and night, for he feared the possibility of theft. His wife, Mandodari, understood the grave mistake her husband had made by abducting Sita in that very flying ship.

"Mandodari had seen Sita's tears and the sorrow etched on her face, her once-glorious eyes red with grief. Sita, the queen of Ayodhya, had become a captive in Ravana's hands, a retaliatory act for the offence committed against his sister, whose ears and nose were severed by Rama's brother, Lakshmana."

"Why did Rama's brother Lakshmana do such a thing to Ravana's sister?"

"Ravana's sister had expressed a desire to marry Lakshmana, but he rejected her proposal and insulted her by cutting off her nose."

"That's too harsh. He didn't have to do that; he could have just refused to marry her."

"A fierce war erupted between the armies of Rama and Ravana. Equally matched in size, strength, and skill, they engaged in a prolonged and indecisive battle that spanned several days. Then, on a fateful day, Rama drew his bowstring and unleashed a formidable arrow that hissed through the air like a serpent, finding its mark in Ravana.

"The powerful weapon pierced Ravana's chest and shattered his limbs, causing him to fall lifeless. In a jubilant chorus, Rama's army erupted in cheers. Learning of her husband's demise, Mandodari, filled with grief, walked into the ocean and took her own life. The remaining Asuras, overwhelmed by defeat, conceded and fled from Lanka." The old woman, Kathika, paused in her storytelling, allowing the weight of the events to sink in.

"Thus came the downfall of Lanka and the Asuras," she murmured, gently swaying back and forth. "King Rama, accompanied by his wife Sita, soared back to Ayodhya aboard the magnificent flying ship. Rama claimed Lanka and expanded the frontiers of his kingdom, solidifying his power.

"Ravana remains suspended between heaven and hell," she went on, her voice filled with soberness. "His soul has found no rest, eternally wandering in the realm of the departed. And as long as the curse of Sita's abduction hangs over us, the Asuras continue to suffer, deprived of peace." Kathika's walking stick struck the ground with a resolute thud, reflecting her anger and frustration.

"As a tribute to our hero, the one and only Ravana," she paused, her voice softened, "the remaining Asuras came together and stole the flying ship from Ayodhya. They concealed the wondrous ship within the heart of the forest, beyond the reach of prying eyes." A gentle smile graced her lips, carrying a hint of secrecy and pride.

"Now, the time of my departure draws near; my days on this earth are numbered. I plead with you to promise that you will safeguard this legendary flying ship."

"We promise," resonated the unified voices of those encircling her.

"I am now prepared to embrace the inevitable end."

Chapter 1
The Murder

> The fire restrains his wonted heat.
> Where stand the dreaded Ravana's feet,
> And, necklaced with the wandering ware,
> The sea before him fears to rave.
>
> —Valmiki Ramayana, Book I, Canto XIV

Year 2000, CE
Beneath the radiant sunlight, Lanka sparkled with an irresistible charm. Tropical trees swayed in the lively wind, their rustling leaves forming a rhythmic symphony. Fishing canoes dotted the waters along the harbour, their sails billowing gracefully. The palm-fringed coastline appeared serene, a picture of tranquillity—but beneath this calm exterior, life and death wove an intricate balance. The Indian Ocean, ancient and unyielding, occasionally revealed her true nature. While she often seemed playful and inviting, there were moments when her ferocity broke through, a stark reminder of her untamed power.

Rohan plunged into the water, snorkelling, and felt an extraordinary transformation take hold, hidden qualities awakened with him, guiding his movements. Like a fish, he seemed to merge seamlessly with the underwater world like he had sprouted gills and fins. Immersed in the rhythmic dance of the waves and cradled by the ocean's depths, a profound euphoria surged through him. The vastness of the sea enveloped him, filling him with an indescribable joy and exhilaration. He relished the freedom, weightlessness and soothing embrace of the underwater world, finding pleasure in the gentle caress of the rocks. Focused on his breath, his heartbeat slowed, leaving behind the problems and worries of dry land.

Curious fish, perceiving him as an outsider, approached with inquisitive gazes. Rohan respectfully reciprocated their curiosity. Lost in the captivating experience of the magnificent underwater world, a sudden realisation snapped him back to reality—he couldn't find his wife, Mira, who had been diving alongside him. Emerging from the depths, driven by the urgency to locate her, he went to the shore.

There, dripping with water, Rohan approached Mira, who was already changing her clothes. "What's wrong? We could have stayed a little longer…" His words carried a mix of confusion and worry, unaware of the reasons for her early return from their shared underwater adventure.

"We must go." She settled herself upon the sandy shore.

Rohan ran his fingers through his damp hair, a sensation of unease gnawing at him. Every time he felt that way, something weird happened. Deep down, a part of him longed for the thrill of another archaeological discovery—mysteries to unravel, challenges to face, and the chance to add another extraordinary adventure to his story.

After changing his clothes, he settled beside Mira and asked, "Have you contacted your father?"

"I tried, but he didn't respond." Her voice tinged with disappointment.

"Are you certain he's in Lanka?"

"Yes, the last time we spoke, he mentioned staying here for a while. He sounded excited and hinted at the success of his research. I'll try to reach him again."

Donning a snug cap and carrying a rucksack, Rohan walked

towards the car, Mira following closely behind. As the sun descended, they climbed into the Ambassador, their mode of transportation. Behind the wheel sat a moustached driver, his face marked by a faint scar. The driver skilfully navigated them to the resort nestled in Ella.

Positioned at the base of Little Adams Peak, the resort had a serene ambience. Its open spaces invited a gentle breeze that brought a welcome coolness to the night air. Their room had a breathtaking panorama with a sweeping view of hills and valleys. Following a delicious dinner, they soon surrendered to sleep, their exhaustion lulling them into a restful slumber.

Inspector Christopher Weerasena was in Colombo when he learnt about the crime near Island Hermitage, the Buddhist monastery on Ratgama Lake. It was a crime that the media spicily called 'Human Sacrifice' and 'The Book Burning Ritual'. There were various puzzling elements in the newspaper. The unidentified body was stabbed to death, with fingers from both hands cut off, and that too on Vijayadashami, a Hindu festival day. Although Chris was born into a Christian family, he knew Lankan Hindus celebrated Vijayadashami—Lord Rama's victory over the Asura-king Ravana. Other reports stated that the murderer had dragged his victim three hundred metres away from the monastery in Galle to a lonely spot in the forest.

According to legend, Galle once had an ancient seaport called Tarshish, where King Solomon traded ivory, peacocks, and other valuables. About two kilometres away from the coast, Chris reached the Buddhist monastery. He shook hands with the uniformed man waiting for him at the lake.

"I am Constable Vijaya." The man saluted. "This way, sir." He led Chris to a boat. The inspector clutched the edge of the wooden seat as the driver started rowing the boat.

"Is this where the murder took place?" Chris asked the constable as the boat headed towards the island.

"Yes, sir."

"Tell me everything you know about the crime, Constable."

"Nothing to say, sir. Journalists have been snooping around, and no one can go closer."

"I don't blame you for that, Constable." Chris pondered and stirred restlessly. "The victim has been stabbed twice, correct? And his fingers were cut off."

"Using an axe or knife, no way to be found, sir."

"Where is the corpse now?" Chris got off the boat and walked towards the forest.

"The body is currently being kept at the nearby hospital, sir. It has been two days since the incident, and I must warn you, the condition is quite distressing."

"Later, I would like to see the body."

"Yes, sir."

"Who found it?"

"One of the monks."

"No one touched the body, correct?"

"No one was allowed, sir."

"Do you know the identification of the victim?"

"The monk knew him as Professor Shastry, sir."

"You don't have to call me sir. What time did the murder take place?"

"Early morning, around six, sir. You are my senior; I must call you sir."

"Can I talk to the monk? The one who first saw the body?"

"He has gone to Colombo for some important work, sir. He assured us he would be back soon."

"And you let him go?" Chris looked at the constable angrily. "Stop calling me sir."

"It's my job, sir. I must call you sir. The poor monk begged and pleaded. His mother was ill, so we let him go."

Chris examined the location of the murder. The contradictory nature of the evidence confused him. Nothing matched. "I have never seen anything like this in my fifty years of life," he said. "Take a sample of this blood. Probably from the victim's body." He removed his glasses, cleaned them, put them on again and let his observant eyes sweep over the burnt papers. Opening his alcohol flask, he offered it to the constable.

"Are you testing me, sir? I don't drink on duty."

Chris ignored the constable's statement and quickly gulped from the flask.

"The murderer was an atheist," the constable alleged.

"Atheist?" Chris questioned swiftly. "What makes you think so?"

"Well, maybe not an atheist exactly," murmured the constable, looking uncomfortable. "I'm a Hindu, sir, and I regularly go to the temple—I better not talk about it anymore. I am just a village constable. I don't know much." He offered his hand, and Chris sat on the boat, leaving the scene.

Amidst the chaotic turmoil swirling around the murder scene, Chris maintained a composed manner as the constable guided him to the local hospital. Journalists and photographers jostled for position, their presence cramming the entrance door. Navigating through the crowd, Chris pressed forward and entered the hospital.

With a steady hand, he lifted the covering from the lifeless figure of a male victim. Adjacent to the table, he observed the blood-stained garments that belonged to the deceased—an ensemble comprising dark trousers, a shirt and sandals. Further examination revealed several articles discovered on the body: a fountain pen, an exquisite timepiece and a cluster of keys. Chris had seen no clues yet and consoled himself with the thought that one could hardly apply logic to the motivations of the seemingly lunatic killer.

Chapter 2
Lanka

> In royal Lanka's glorious town
> A city bright and rich, that showed
> Well-ordered streets and noble roads
> Arranged with just division, fair
> With multitudes in court and square.
> —Valmiki Ramayana, Book III, Canto LIV

With the dawn of a new day, Rohan went to Badulla, a town nestled upon the eastern slopes of Lanka. Surrounded by the majestic Nine-Peak mountain range and encircled by the Oya River, Badulla held its significance. Legend had it that after attaining Nirvana, the Buddha, accompanied by five hundred disciples, graced the sacred grounds of the Maha Vihara Temple in Badulla. Adjacent to this revered temple stood one of the oldest archaeological sites in all of Lanka, carrying the weight of historical wonders and ancient treasures.

"I am Priya Das, professor of archaeology," a slender and dusky woman approached Rohan. "Welcome to Lanka. I'm delighted that you can join us."

"Thank you for the invitation," Rohan said.

"Is your hotel comfortable?"

"Oh, yes. It's a lovely place."

The woman lifted her hat momentarily before allowing it to rest beneath her chin. Her face showed elegance, sparkling eyes and a thin-lipped smile that displayed warmth.

"Let me take you on a tour," she offered, leading him

towards the temple. "The buried temple," she said, "appears as an extension of the existing one. The excavation in Badulla has been ongoing for many years. The site suffered damages even before Lanka gained independence from the British. Additionally, it has been subjected to looting on several occasions."

"When was this site initially discovered?" he asked, following closely behind her, eager for further insights.

"It was first discovered in 1900. During those turbulent times of the struggle for independence, many valuable artefacts disappeared from the old temple. We lack sufficient documentation," she explained.

The uniquely designed temple had six levels. Its external walls were embellished with intricate depictions of dragon heads, bulls, peacocks, lion sculptures, a small Buddha statue, and other elements commonly associated with Buddhist temples. The entrance showcased a vibrant display of artistry, ornamental terracotta bricks and arched panels. Every aspect of the temple, from its walls, wainscot and ceiling to its doors, shutters and fences, was meticulously constructed within a sturdy framework to provide structural support. As they ventured inside the dome-shaped stone structure, they were greeted by the expansive prayer hall.

"Do you know what happened to the main statue of the Buddha?" Rohan inquired.

"Based on our investigations," she explained, "we have reason to believe that in 1920, a German anthropologist named Egon von Eickstedt, who was here to study the human race, might have taken with him. Eickstedt's study was highly controversial."

"Ms Das, I thought our destination was the coastal line?"

"Please, call me Priya. Our original plan was to head towards the coastal line. The driver will take you to the Godawaya site, approximately a hundred and forty kilometres from here. Our team of archaeologists made a remarkable discovery of underwater artefacts. We require your expertise in deep diving to retrieve these objects from the ocean."

It was a bright day with a cool breeze blowing over the coastal line. At a distance from the archaeological site, fisherfolk prepared boats to start at the turn of the tide. Rohan studied the open sea wind pattern, observing the boat movements. The archaeologists hired three fibre boats to inspect the site underwater. Without any harbour, they had to push the boats into the sea manually. The exploration team included divers and marine archaeologists.

Rohan placed two markers over the site, which served as shot lines for the diver's entry and exit. Using a rope with a measuring tape attached, he set up a fifty-metre baseline on a bearing of three hundred degrees. He divided the length into three divisions that served as the teams' respective areas of assignment.

One team was tasked with photographing artefacts using two digital cameras. Underwater cameras were used to record on-site activities. A second team documented the mound of metal strips on the northern side of the baseline. Based on the data collected, they created a site map. With the help of his team, Rohan conducted detailed mapping and photography using open-circuit scuba and wireless communication. About thirty-one metres down into the ocean, he discovered substantial metal pieces scattered in bits and pieces of different shapes and sizes. He took pictures of the artefacts. A live underwater video was established to transmit the digitised signal to the shore.

At first, Rohan thought it was a shipwreck. Carefully looking at the largest intact piece of metal, he realised that it couldn't be a ship but something else. What he saw astonished him. Could it be the relics of a plane crash? With the help of a crane, the team lifted the larger metal pieces to the land. He had to wait until he returned to the laboratory to learn more.

Due to the absence of a decompression chamber on the site, dive bottom time was limited to eighteen minutes, the maximum time allowed for a no-decompression dive. It was already the twentieth minute. His colleagues were signalling him to come back to the shore. Before he swam back, he took one last look at the ocean from within but found nothing more.

After changing his clothes, Rohan rested on the sandy beach for a while, looking admiringly at the sea. At a distance from where he sat, lush green coconut trees provided shade to the huts with their thatched roofs that housed restaurants. To his right was a forest with ancient trees. Millions of years ago, Lanka had been part of the mainland of the Indian subcontinent. Based on geological evidence, it is suggested that the sunken bridge in the northwestern part of the island was once a land connection between India and Lanka.

At a distance, a young woman stood watching him. She wore jeans and a T-shirt. Her skin was dusky like the night. She stood calm but with the restlessness of a fighter and the keen eyes of a spy.

The shore was quiet except for the archaeological team and fisherfolk who drew in their nets at the fading tide. He noticed the woman walking towards him. She had sharp jaws, long hair tied up on her crown in a bunch, seashell ornaments around her neck and hands, a wooden boomerang and a scalping knife held in her girdle. It seemed as if she had known hardships and exertion from her earliest youth. She spoke to him using a language with which he was unfamiliar.

"I don't understand your language," Rohan admitted.

"It is a flying machine," she said in English. Her nose rings touched her lips as she spoke. "The ocean has treasures in it, a lot of treasures. The big-size thing you found in the water has a true story."

"How do you know what we found?" he asked her. A crow cawed in the distance.

"Do you know that some can read what one has seen? Do you understand that what you have seen, some can explain better? I am a seer, and I can do that."

"You mean that you could tell what I saw simply by looking at my face?"

"Not everything, but I know what you have found underwater today."

"There are too many seers in this world, don't you think so?"

"The spirit speaks only into the chosen ears, and the vision solely comes to the chosen eyes." There was something fearful in the woman's eyes. The crow cawed louder than before.

"Why did the spirit choose you?" Rohan moved away from her.

"You don't believe me. Do you? This is the work of fate." Her necklace had the shape of a peacock head.

"Then perhaps you should tell me what you saw and how."

"Do not worry about that. All I can tell you is that it was no coincidence. When the spirit speaks, there is no more chance. Be sure to be like the night, which always follows the day. Fate knows their wishes and their work, blind or not, sane or insane, but fate does."

"Your belief must have come from some ancient tradition, am I right?"

"You should think about yourself," she whispered. "I have seen the sea ruffle without a cause. I have heard deathly cries. You will also see that..." She stopped suddenly as though interfered with some thoughts in her mind.

"What else did the spirit tell you?"

"Nothing more," she said. Her eyes were red like on fire as if instincts were guiding her thoughts in a strange way. She sat down on the sand, looking towards the sea, silently watching the rise and fall of the waves, seemingly concerned or worried about something. She moved her right hand across her forehead as though to clear her thoughts. "The voice has spoken," she announced, "and what it has said will be. Some stand in the way of fate and try to hinder the coming. Nevertheless, it is going to happen. They can no longer block the flow of time." Her words seemed to come from another world.

"What voice is it? Anything I can understand?"

The crow continued cawing.

"Do not question the working of the Almighty," she warned him. "Do not question fate." Once or twice, she seemed as though she was about to speak and tell more but hesitated.

"I am curious. Please don't mistake me."

After a while, she said with an effort, "The voice speaks in sounds heard by the inner ear. I can hear those words, and my brain understands them. Not many can hear the inner voice. I cannot explain my methods. I have powers of my own." Her brows wrinkled up in thought. Her face showed how serious she was. She looked around like a hunted animal, chased by someone or something.

"I see you searching for the Old World," she continued. "What's the point? You will find it only to be taken away again. You must believe in the sun, the moon and my words. For ages, the voice has spoken to people I know, and it has never failed. I must warn you. It is not safe for you to be here. You should go back to your home at once. Go back to the place where you come from. Go home. Do not meddle with old things, they have a troubled soul hidden in them." Saying so, she walked away towards the coconut trees, leaving behind long strides on the beach.

When he looked at her again, she was suddenly gone, as if the wind had taken her away. All he could see in her place was a cat walking, which turned around to look at Rohan. Did she just turn into a cat? He smiled at his own foolish thoughts but surprisingly looked at the cat again. The unusual words of the young woman seemed strange without any logic. She appeared entangled in her own world, a world which he couldn't understand.

Rohan walked back to his team. The artefacts were ready for transportation to the laboratory in Badulla. Rohan sat in the car that escorted the pickup truck. All through the way, he pondered about the artefacts. This could be the greatest of all findings.

Chapter 3
The Professor

I will not close my slumbering eyes,
Till by this hand my foeman dies.
And when mine arm has slain the foe
Who laid those giant princes low,
Long will I triumph in the deed,
Like one enriched in utmost need.

—Valmiki Ramayana, Book III, Canto LIV

The archaeology department was located in a building on the far side of the square in Badulla. In a room with large windows, the administration staff had doubled since the beginning of the excavation. The offices were confidently known as *temporary* and labourers had been contracted to demolish the old building to make way for a new office block.

Rohan settled himself on the chair, drew a necklace out of his pocket and placed it on the desk between Priya and him. It had the shape of a peacock head, about ten centimetres long, flat, thin, and made of gold with a crude design.

Priya picked it up, weighed the necklace in her palm, looked at it carefully, and said, "Where did you find it?"

"Underwater," he replied.

"Strange, especially the way it looks," Priya said, dropping her voice to a whisper. "I am pretty sure this belongs to the Asuras."

"Asuras, the enemies of the gods?"

"Yes, Rohan. They are believed to have descended from the same lineage as the ancient Asuras mentioned in the Vedas, often associated with darkness and chaos. I have also heard they are greedy, seeking power, wealth and pleasure."

"Well, I didn't know they still existed—the modern-day Asuras."

"All I know is that there's an indigenous group of people who call themselves the Asuras. I have only heard of them, never met them."

"Priya, what makes you believe this necklace belongs to them?"

"Our team had discovered a thousand-year-old necklace as stunning as this one, made of gold, rubies, turquoise and other precious stones. It was found on the body of a powerful woman buried in Ravana's cave in Ella. They say she belonged to the high society, a leader, a queen or a princess. Inside the cave, we have found evidence of ancient rituals. I will hand this necklace to our anthropologist. It will be a listed item and the credit goes to you, Rohan."

Rohan's phone rang. "Hello?" he answered.

"I have been trying to contact you all day," Mira panicked. "But you didn't answer my calls."

"What's wrong? Are you okay?"

"Terrible news…My father is dead. He's been murdered."

"What! How do you know?"

Mira lost her voice for a second but recovered nervously. "It's in the newspapers, with his photograph."

"Did you call the police?"

"Yes, I did."

"What did they say?"

"They want me to identify the body."

"Wait for me, I will be there soon." He hung up the phone.

Rohan came to the hotel and picked up Mira to take her to the hospital in Galle. Mira sat still in the car, traumatised. She was not very communicative during the long drive. She couldn't believe that her father was dead. Sensing her nervousness, he held her hand, trying to make her feel better.

At the hospital, they met Inspector Christopher Weerasena, who led them to the mortuary. "Can you identify this unfortunate man?" he asked, showing the body that lay on the table.

Mira nervously looked at the body. "He is my father," she said.

"My condolences for your loss, madam," Chris said. "Please wait for me in the lobby, and I will join you shortly."

Tears streamed down her face and she sobbed. "I'll never get to see him again."

Rohan held Mira's hand, offering comfort.

Inspector Chris took a seat. "I understand this is a difficult time for you, but I need to ask you a few questions."

"Please tell me, inspector. Who killed my father and why?"

"We don't have that information yet, but we are investigating. A Buddhist monk discovered his body in the forest near the Island Hermitage. Your father was fatally stabbed in the chest with a knife, and I regret to inform you that his fingers were severed before his demise," Chris explained like he was describing damages caused to a car in an accident.

"Who could commit such a heinous act? What could have driven someone to do something so brutal? And why was my father on that island?" Her voice quivered.

"We will keep you updated as and when we find out," Inspector Chris reassured her. "Now, if you don't mind, I would like to ask you a few questions. What was your father's name?"

"Professor Anant Ram Shastry," she replied.

"When did he arrive in Lanka?"

"I don't know. When I spoke to him a month ago, he was already in Lanka."

"His official residence is in India, correct?"

"Yes, that's correct."

"What about your mother? Professor Shastry's wife?"

"My mother passed away two years ago," she replied.

"How did she die?"

"She died of cancer."

"Any idea why your father came here?"

"He mentioned that he was doing some research. He seemed quite enthusiastic about his findings," she replied.

"Do you have any suspicion who might be responsible for his murder?" Chris probed.

"No," she said.

"When did you arrive in Lanka?" was his next question.

"We arrived on Saturday."

"Why are both of you here?"

"I am currently writing an article on Lanka. My husband, Rohan, was invited by the archaeology department for an underwater project," she explained.

"Ah, I've heard about the excavations. So, do you go underwater in the ocean to discover artefacts?" Chris looked at Rohan.

"Yes," answered Rohan.

"And why do you do that? This question is only out of my curiosity."

"Isn't it fascinating to discover something that drowned many years ago? Don't you want to know what lies beneath? My role, Officer, is to gather evidence and tell stories of times long before ours," Rohan replied.

"How exciting!" Chris said cynically. "Are you also a deep-sea diver, madam?" He turned to Mira.

"Yes, I am. When I'm not writing, I'm exploring underwater," Mira responded.

"A writer who deep dives." Chris noted down in his book. "How did you learn about your father's death?"

"From the newspaper this morning," she answered.

"Is that so?" Chris said, examining them closely. "Here's my card. Contact me if you need any assistance."

"How long will the body be kept, Officer?" Rohan asked.

"We have to wait for the post-mortem reports," Chris replied.

A clerk from the mortuary approached them. "Please sign these," he said, handing the papers to Mira. "They are no-objection papers."

Mira signed the papers.

They sat in the hospital lobby for a while, trying to come to terms with Professor Shastry's sudden death. "I always sensed that something like this could happen to him," Mira said.

"Why do you say that?"

"I never knew where my father was or what he was doing. I wish he had been more communicative with me, but he was always engrossed in his work, a man who loved his job. And now, look where it has led him," she said sadly.

"I think we should go," Rohan suggested, and they walked out of the hospital. "Please take us to the hotel," he instructed the driver.

"The last time I saw him was in Nice, France," Mira recalled. "Whenever we met, our conversations were more practical than affectionate. He would share stories about new artefacts he had discovered or the classes he was teaching, but he couldn't remember my birthday and openly acknowledged it. It surprised me when he called me last month. That was a rarity. He mentioned he was doing research and writing a book on Ravana. I asked him why Ravana, as it is an ancient and well-known tale. He insisted it was a different story, a retelling of history from the perspective of the renowned Lankan monarch.

"From what I gathered, my father intended to delve into what happened to Ravana and his family after the Lankan War. He wanted to unveil the untold aspects of Valmiki's epic, *The Ramayana*. I find it puzzling: Who would want to harm my father? Who would hold a grudge against a historian? And why would someone hate him, torture him and take his life? Such an unexpected tragedy! And then, there's the baffling act of severing his finger. I need to find out who did it and why?"

The sun began to set when Mira and Rohan reached their hotel in Badulla. Weary from a long day and emotionally shaken by the loss of Professor Shastry, Mira and Rohan went to their room. Rohan quickly fell asleep. Mira couldn't sleep. She tried to read a red-cover novel, but the storyline felt feeble in comparison to the profound mystery she was grappling with. Her mind incessantly wandered back to her deceased father, keeping her in a state of restlessness throughout the night. It wasn't until the early hours of the morning that sleep finally overcame her.

Chapter 4
The Buddhist Monk

A cry from earth rose long and shrill,
The wind hushed; the sun grew chill.
The thunder bellowed from the sky,
And troubled ocean roared reply.

—Valmiki Ramayana, Book V, Canto XLVII

Buddhist monk Assaji guided Inspector Chris through the corridors until they reached Professor Shastry's room. The inspector's mind was brimming with extraordinary thoughts, which he kept to himself. Constable Vijaya followed them.

The room resembled a library, with an extensive collection of books lined up on shelves. Beneath the window stood a table, and the stone floor was covered by a vibrant carpet. Against one wall, a neatly made bed added comfort to the scholarly atmosphere.

"Did Professor Shastry spend a lot of time here?" Chris asked, looking at the monk.

"This was his room for the past three years. He used to come and go," the monk responded.

Inspector Chris went closer to the writing table. Hidden underneath a pile of papers in the bin was a laptop, deliberately smashed into several pieces before being discarded. Realising the potential importance of this finding, he directed, "Vijaya, take this bin with you and gather any fingerprints you can find."

Chris continued to examine the room. He opened the drawers to find them filled with papers. "It seems Professor Shastry was engaged in some research," he said.

"I don't know about that," said the monk. "He was deeply involved in his work, although he chose to keep the specifics to himself."

"Have you noticed anything out of the ordinary or encountered any unfamiliar faces in your neighbourhood?"

"No, Officer, I haven't."

"I assume that the Island Hermitage is typically a tranquil place. The presence of any new individuals would likely stir up gossip, correct?" Chris probed further.

"Yes, that's a possibility, although we do have tourists visiting the area quite frequently,"

"And where were you at the time of the murder, Mr Assaji?"

"I was away in Colombo, giving a lecture."

"Are you the only one here? It seems deserted today." Chris noted.

"There are ten people who live here, but they are travelling monks who move from one monastery to another, either teaching or pursuing further knowledge," Assaji explained.

"How well acquainted were you with Professor Shastry?" was his next question.

"Not very well. I knew him to be kind-hearted and friendly, but he was always absorbed in his books and papers."

"Is there anything you can share that might shed new light on the case?" Chris pressed.

"A gentleman from Germany visited Professor Shastry a few days before his demise. He stayed here for some time. Perhaps you can gather some information from him," Assaji revealed.

"Do you know his name?"

"Professor Shastry introduced him to me as Arthur Hoffmann, a friend."

"How would you describe Arthur Hoffmann's appearance?"

"He was tall, blond, with a distinctive nose, and dressed in expensive clothes. He rarely interacted with anyone besides Professor Shastry. They would sit together for hours, engrossed in discussions that sometimes escalated into arguments," Assaji recounted.

"What were they arguing about?"

"I'm not sure."

"Could you show me the room where Arthur Hoffmann stayed?"

"It's the adjacent room," Assaji said, walking towards it. As he produced a bunch of keys from his pocket and unlocked the door, he added, "This is where he stayed."

"Has anyone accessed this room since Hoffmann left?"

"No, but it was cleaned after he departed," Assaji informed.

"I can smell cigars. Did Hoffmann smoke cigars?"

"Yes, whenever I saw him, he had a cigar in his mouth," Assaji confirmed.

Inspector Chris meticulously examined the surroundings. A sense of foreboding lingered in the air, contrasting with the serene beauty of the sunlit garden outside. It was difficult to believe that beneath this peaceful façade lay a disturbing murder mystery.

"I suggest you remain vigilant," Inspector Chris advised the monk. "If you come across anything suspicious, contact me immediately."

Assaji nodded in agreement.

"We will gather all the things that belonged to Professor Shastry. Vijaya, please pack them carefully, ensuring the preservation of any fingerprints," Chris instructed.

Inspector Chris and Vijaya departed from the monastery with two large boxes in tow, leaving behind a house overshadowed by an unsettling tragedy.

Chapter 5
In the Laboratory

> The prize which Ravana seized of old
> Victorious o'er the God of Gold
> This chariot, kept with utmost care,
> Will waft thee through the fields of air,
> And thou shalt light unwearied down
> In fair Ayodhya's royal town.
>
> —Valmiki Ramayana, Book III, Canto LIV

Priya Das tended to the metal plates immersed in the expansive desalination pool. She looked up at Rohan as he entered the room and greeted him, "Good morning." Priya had an aura of calmness as if surrounded by a shield that protected her from any disturbance. "You look exhausted," she said. "Have you been lost in thoughts about our recent discovery, trying to make sense of it all?"

"Not only that but there are other confusing matters weighing on my mind. I'm currently mourning the tragic loss of my father-in-law, Professor Shastry. He was brutally murdered," Rohan revealed, his voice tinged with sorrow.

"You're referring to the murder in Galle? The killing of Professor Anant Ram Shastry, your father-in-law?"

"Yes, that's exactly what I am talking about. Did you know him?"

"I knew him well. He was an exceptional man. I'm so sorry for your loss. The news of his demise is horrifying,"

"Priya, did you meet Professor Shastry while he was in Lanka?"

"Yes, I had the privilege of meeting him twice recently. In fact, it was Professor Shastry who suggested that you could assist me with the archaeological work. You see, I was his student during my university days, and our recent meetings revolved around his new book on Ravana and the Asuras. He knew of my previous research on Ravana's flying object, so we got together to discuss some archaeological findings. He had a profound influence on my career. My heartfelt condolences to you and your wife. I'm certain Professor Shastry would have been delighted to know about our recent discovery."

"Why didn't you mention this earlier?"

"Well, I suppose I didn't consider it relevant then."

"His body remained unidentified until yesterday. Why didn't you notify the authorities or provided your testimony if you knew him?"

"I should have, but I couldn't bring myself to do it. Since losing my husband, I find it incredibly difficult to confront the sight of a lifeless body. That's why I refrained from informing the police."

"I'm so sorry to hear about your husband—that's heartbreaking. When did he pass away?"

"Two years ago. But the pain still feels fresh. Life goes on, doesn't it?"

Continuing her work, she checked the salinity levels using a specialised instrument. She skilfully removed any remnants of deposits, employing a mechanical scalpel and power chisel.

Although Rohan's thoughts still lingered on Professor Shastry, he focused his attention on a sizeable fragment of the artefact. Together, they carefully washed it by hand, as it was too large for either of them to handle alone. With Priya holding one end, he removed deposits, encrusted sea organisms, and iron oxides from the surface using specialised chemicals.

Subsequently, they submerged the fragments in a solution of hydrochloric acid and water, followed by rinsing in running water. They employed a solution of vinyl dissolved in acetone, along with electrochemical cleaning, to eliminate any remaining surface film and electrolyte layer. After another round of rinsing and drying, the brightly shining artefact revealed its true splendour.

Next, they subjected it to ultrasound and laser cleaning, followed by UV and X-ray photography to capture detailed images and gather additional information about its composition and structure. Each step of the process was executed with precision and care, revealing new insights into the remarkable artefact they had discovered.

"It's a miracle," Priya said, marvelling at its condition. "How are these artefacts not prone to rusting or cracks?"

They carefully arranged the metal pieces together in a cylindrical shape resembling the rear part of an aircraft. Although its size was similar to that of a helicopter, its design defied any modern machine.

"The carbon tests are here," Priya said, looking at the report. "They have confirmed that the metal object dates to the early twentieth century. Even more remarkable is that the alloy used in its construction is unknown, making it truly unique." She left the laboratory momentarily and returned with a file in her hand. "Look at this, Rohan," she said. "We have discovered similar metal fragments during previous expeditions."

"How interesting!" he said, looking at the report.

"Some years back," Priya recounted, "a farmer discovered a wooden pipe lying in a bush near the coastal line. A few steps later, he found a pair of broken glasses that looked like a binocular. And he caught the sight of a notebook. The owner of the farm sent it to the archaeological department. It belonged to Shivkar Bapuji Talpade, a qualified aeronaut who built this flying machine. He was from Maharashtra in India. Born in 1845, he was a man of considerable wealth, much of which he had spent in pursuing his aeronautical hobby.

"The notebook," she said, taking another hardcover from the shelf, "is here. Some pages are missing. However, the pages that survived are mostly readable. It is written in Marathi, his native language. He refers to instructions given in the Vaimanika Shastra, a Sanskrit version of the aeronautical science, to build his machine. In his own words, Talpade explains what he experienced while building it and the thoughts that went through his mind as he climbed the flying machine." Priya leafed through the pages.

"According to entries in his notebook," she continued, "just before the clouds had obscured his view, the flying machine suddenly rose perpendicularly upwards in a succession of jerks. On the last page, which appears like he has jotted down in a hurry from a moving airplane, is hardly legible. He writes: *God help me; it is a dreadful way to die*. Those were his final words.

"The notebook has stains, both on the last page and on the outside cover, which the experts have pronounced to be human blood. He must have fallen from a great height in a tremendous speed and died in the crash in 1900. When the farm-owner found his body in the rice fields, his head was obliterated, as if he had fallen from high altitude."

"Three years before the Wright Brothers invented their aircraft," Rohan remarked, tapping his finger on the table.

Priya searched the bookshelf for a while and held out another paperback. "Rohan," she said, "we have also with us the Vaimanika Shastra, written in Sanskrit in 1818 by Pundit Subbaraya Shastry. Vaimanika Shastra has three thousand hymns similar to the ancient

Vedic style of writing. The book begins with the description of a flying machine. The following chapters include a definition of flying, on pilots, aerial routes, food, clothing, metals, metal production, mirrors and their uses, varieties of machinery. The book describes four distinct types of machines in detail along with diagrams, namely—*Shankuna*, *Tripura*, *Sundara* and *Rukma*."

"So," Rohan added, "we have two volumes here. One, a notebook that states Talpade built a flying machine, which he flew before he died. What we lifted from the Indian Ocean is part of Talpade's flying machine. Talpade refers to have used Vaimanika Shastra to build his machine. Two, we have Vaimanika Shastra, the Sanskrit manuscript. That sounds great, doesn't it? I need a smoke." He went outside, lit his cigarette and stared at the tree with the air of someone whose imagination and ideas were formulating in his mind.

Priya stood next to him.

He slowly exhaled smoke and uttered something that sounded like an abrupt laugh. "I'm impressed, Professor Priya. You've began to reconstruct the hypotheses on the flying machine. This is turning into something absolutely interesting."

"The topic wasn't entirely unfamiliar to me. I have been working on this subject for a long time. One question that captivated me to keep going was, is it true that there existed a flying machine during ancient times? With no evidence so far, this question remained unanswered. Now, we have some proof. The artefact we lifted from the ocean can be one of its unique kind based on the Vaimanika Shastra."

"There was a time," she continued, "when the topic of ancient flying machines was fashionable."

"Priya, tell me, did you discuss all this with Professor Anant Ram Shastry?"

"Yes, I did," she replied.

"I can see things coming together—the discovery of the artefact, the death of Professor Shastry, and the tales of the flying machine. I feel there's something more to it, though I'm not sure what." He took a deep drag on his cigarette, and asked, "Tell me, how long have you been at this site in Badulla?"

"About six months. I came here for this project."

"Where were you before that?"

"I am a teacher at the University of Heidelberg in Germany. Lanka is where I was born. I never say no when I get a chance to come here and stay in my homeland, even if it is for a brief period. I don't know why but the Vaimanika Shastra has been haunting me for years."

After Priya had locked the premises, they both walked together towards the car park.

"I have an odd sense of uneasiness. The same feeling I had as a young boy standing atop a towering building, mustering the courage to gaze down at the ground," Rohan added.

"There's something else that's troubling me," Priya said. "It's about the murder of Professor Shastry and that of my husband. My husband was a journalist. Artefacts, antique, historical object and history were his favourite topics.

"One day, he received an invitation to attend an auction of South Asian artefacts that was to take place in Berlin. There, he found ancient copper plates. They were priceless. He couldn't resist buying them.

"During those days, I was busy with my PhD. He took the copper plates and travelled to Lanka to get them deciphered by a Sinhalese expert. I really do not know what happened after that. I got the news of his death. I at once flew here."

"I can only imagine what you must have endured. What's

your husband's name?"

"Davis Ranatunga."

"Who killed him?"

"The investigation is still going on. I fear I may never know why my husband died or who killed him. What I wanted to tell you is that Davis was murdered in a similar fashion to Professor Shastry."

"Who is investigating your husband's case?"

"Inspector Christopher Weerasena," Priya answered.

"He is also looking into Professor Shastry's murder case. Do you know what happened to the copper plates?"

"When I met Professor Shastry, he informed me that he had the copper plates. He mentioned that my husband had given them to him."

After bidding farewell to Priya, Rohan settled into the car. The driver chauffeured him back to the hotel while raindrops cascaded down the windowpane. Amidst flashes of lightning and thunderous roars in the sky, the tinkling of a small cluster of brass bells hanging from the rear-view mirror filled the air.

When he stepped out of the car at the hotel, raindrops splashed on his face and trickled into his collar—a welcome relief from the tropical heat. Still, his mind remained consumed by the double murder, suspecting the same individual was responsible for both crimes.

Chapter 6
The Email

His threatening brows so darkly frowned,
His eyes so fiercely glanced around,
They made his glare, which none might brook,
Like some infuriate lion's look.
—*Valmiki Ramayana*, Book II, Canto XXIII

Upon entering the hotel room, Rohan noticed Mira's absence. A note she had left behind assured him of her return. He turned on some music, undressed, and stepped into the shower, leaving the bathroom door open to allow the soothing notes of a classical piano to accompany him.

The room, filled with music, created a barrier between him and the outside world. After showering, he wrapped himself in a towel, poured a glass of wine, and settled onto the sofa, contemplating the artefact that he had discovered. His imagination filled in the missing pieces, stirring an emotional connection.

Throughout his professional life, he held onto a core belief that no discovery could fully explain reality, but rather offer only fleeting glimpses into the past. Resting on the sofa, he closed his eyes, enveloped by the music coming from the player. He focused on deep, steady breaths, attempting to dispel the momentary worry that had crossed his mind—where could Mira possibly be?

He fell into a deep sleep and was immersed in a vivid dream—a strange journey aboard a flying machine in search of Mira. In this ethereal world, he sat among ancient aviators, soaring above the vast expanse of the Indian Ocean. The tranquillity was abruptly shattered as the aircraft plummeted in a catastrophic crash. A haunting sense of death hung heavily in the air, wrapping him in its grip. Echoes of screams rose from the desperate souls within the ill-fated flight. Suddenly, a man stood from his seat, brandishing a knife and mercilessly attacking the other passengers, severing their fingers. Cries to God and their loved ones echoed through the cabin.

Upon awakening, it took him a moment to regain his composure. A cigarette clutched between his lips, he tried to strike a match, but his trembling hand betrayed him as if he had brushed against the face of death. Finally, he lit the cigarette and poured himself another measure of wine.

Mira entered the room with a bundle of papers in her hand. Her face radiant with excitement, she said. "You won't believe what I found today!"

"What did you find?" he asked.

"My father's research papers and his unfinished book."

"Where did you get them?"

"He had sent me an email the day before he was murdered. It seems like he had sensed some danger."

"Did he leave any message in his email?"

"There was no message, only these attachments. I read a few pages. My father was quite the storyteller. I feel obliged to complete his unfinished work."

"Be careful. We must disclose this only to those we trust."

Mira's attention was drawn to photographs showcasing ancient copper plates. "I wonder where he found these," she murmured.

"He got these from my colleague Priya's husband. Priya is one of the archaeologists I work with. Apparently, her husband bought these copper plates at an auction in Berlin and later gave them to Professor Shastry. These photographs look like the same plates."

"So, Priya knew my father."

"Yes, there's a peculiar connection between how your father and her husband met their tragic ends."

"The case is getting more complex," she stated.

"We should talk to Priya and discuss these photographs with her."

Rohan held the papers in this hand and read the words penned by Professor Shastry:

In the beginning, there was only darkness. In this state of emptiness, nothing existed, neither moving nor static. Then came cosmic water. Within the water, Svayambu, the self-born arose. It created a seed within itself. The seed turned into a golden womb. Hiranyagarbha was born. Gods came from the golden womb. They divided the world into three parts: heaven, earth and underworld.

The universe enveloped in its shells compelled by the wheel of time, infinite, repeating itself, in a cyclical motion of creation and destruction. Humans occupied the earth. The Asuras were born from Yama, the god of death. The Asuras became their own creators, destroyers, protectors.

The woman who narrated this story was Kali, the chief of the Asuras. She ruled the underworld—the Yamaloka, where the Asuras lived. Her father was Andhaka, the dark one. He was a proud Asura. Kali's mother was Danu, who lived underwater.

Andhaka and Danu had three children—Jambava, Naga, and Kali. Kali's bones on one side of her face were fully exposed. No one could hide anything from Kali. She had an eye of fire, which could see the truth, and ears that could hear like a moth. She lived in a place hot like fire.

"Yes, it's hard," Kali said. "Today, even in the twenty-first century, in these hurrying and fragmented times, it's hard to be *an Asura. I am in constant burning agony as if my whole body is on fire. My face, oh my face, is only half,"* she lamented, full of rage.

"The other half of my face was taken away by flames that burned for months. My vision is restricted to one eye only. And who, you may ask, is to blame for that? Did I choose my fate?" she argued. *"Wasn't everything hunky-dory in this world? Before I burnt, that was, when I had my full face, I looked like Ravana, the great. That's partly why I had been chosen to be the chief of the Asuras, because of my face.*

"Then Yama sent his men to seize the children of Andhaka and bring them to him. Those men appeared before the family and threw our brother, Naga the serpent, into the deep sea. But our brother grew so large, out in the middle of the ocean, he coiled around the whole of Lanka, biting his own tail.

"They threw the other brother, Jambava, into the forest and made him the ruler. They threw me into the underworld and made me its ruler. That's where we are, in this enormous dwelling we have built together within the walls of immense height and the huge gates. We called the place Yamaloka. Yama did all this to gain our love, to make us rulers," Kali said.

"Yamaloka is a realm of fire and heat, close to the Indian Ocean. Hot and glowing land of fire, home of the Asuras, and guarded by Kali with her flaming sword. Yamaloka was the first place that was made on earth. The sparks from the fire created the sun, moon and star," explained Kali.

Chapter 7
The Flying Machine

> The broad-winged rover of the skies.
> O Rama, haste, thine aid I crave:
> O Lakshman, why delay to save?
> Brave sons of old Ikshvaku, hear
> And rescue in this hour of fear.
>
> —Valmiki Ramayana, Book III, Canto LII

"It's a real flying machine," affirmed Sunil De Silva, aeronautical engineer. "It appears quite plausible despite its age," he said, brushing his fingers against his moustache. With frizzy hair and dark skin, he bore a resemblance to an Asian version of Albert Einstein.

"From every perspective, the evidence strongly suggests that this is the remains of a flying machine," he said, gazing at the artefacts and seemingly lost in thoughts. "To be honest, I'm not sure how much assistance I can offer you."

"The main question we have is," Rohan began, "whether this thing could actually fly. There are two significant reasons behind our curiosity. First, if it could fly, it would provide evidence of the flying machine predating the Wright Brothers' invention of aeroplanes. Second, it would lend support to the notion that this manuscript here describes the ancient aeronautical science mentioned by Talpade, who tragically died while piloting his machine."

As Sunil stood among archaeologists and faced the artefact, his initial unease dissipated, replaced by a fascination for the machine before him. He studied it, examining its exterior and interior, taking measurements, and walking around it.

Requesting some papers and a pencil, he thoughtfully contemplated before leaning on the table to sketch the artefact. Briefly leaving his drawing aside, he took a closer look at the artefact and remarked, "If the person who constructed this followed modern principles, we might be able to draw some conclusions. Otherwise, deciphering will become more challenging."

"How could you determine if this machine was able to fly?" Rohan questioned.

"We need to consider two significant concepts in aerodynamics: continuum and drag, both of which were discussed by Aristotle. Sir Isaac Newton also made significant contributions to the theory of air resistance. Drag is influenced by the body's dimensions, fluid density, and velocity squared. These factors have proven to be particularly accurate when dealing with low flow speeds.

"Newton formulated a law to calculate the drag force on a flat plate when it's inclined in the direction of fluid flow. We use symbols such as F for the drag force, ρ for density, S for the plate's area, V for flow velocity, and θ for the inclination angle. The law can be expressed as $F = \rho S V^2 \sin^2(\theta)$. There's the lift equation, which states $L = k \, S \, V^2 \, C_L$."

"I'm completely lost," Rohan admitted, looking at Priya. "How about you?"

"Rocket science," Priya replied, puzzled.

"Based on what I see here," Sunil said, "I can offer a probable conclusion on whether this object could fly."

"Sunil, how much time do you need?" Rohan inquired.

"I'm not certain. Half an hour, a week, or maybe longer," Sunil replied, scratching his ill-shaven chin. "It depends on how well I can focus on the problem. I'd like to create a probabilistic model and assess it."

"Here, look at this book," Rohan said, handing it to him. "It's the Vaimanika Shastra, translated into English. The book supposedly describes the ancient flying machine. Can you start examining it right away?"

"Of course, I already have," Sunil replied.

After Sunil left, Rohan immersed himself in reading the ancient tales of flying objects. He delved into the report in front of him, seeking clues that could unlock the mysteries surrounding these ancient phenomena.

The people of ancient Bharat used flying objects for warfare. The epic Ramayana vividly recounts a fearsome war that occurred thousands of years ago, involving astonishing weapons of destruction that were unimaginable until the latter half of the twentieth century.

The Mahabharata describes the devastating power of war, with a weapon likened to a single projectile charged with the energy of the entire universe.

The Mahabharata offers a treasure trove of information regarding conflicts between gods, who engaged in battles using lethal weapons and blazing missiles.

For instance, the 'Indra's Dart' operated with a circular 'reflector' and emitted a focused 'shaft of light' capable of instantly consuming its target with its immense power.

In one episode, Lord Krishna pursued his enemy, Salva, in the sky, and despite Salva's attempt to conceal his flying object, the Saubha, Krishna skilfully employed a special weapon guided by sound to defeat him.

The Mahabharata chronicle the usage of the Iron Thunderbolt, leaving its victims unrecognisable and causing their hair and nails to fall out.

Rohan lit a cigarette. The authors of the Ramayana and Mahabharata seemed as if they had actually witnessed these events, they vividly describe. The Vedas, written thousands of years ago, also mentioned flying objects. Why would someone write about things they had never seen or experienced? Imagination can only flourish with prior knowledge, and creative ideas are born from facts and personal experience.

"A puzzling flying machine," Rohan murmured to himself, feeling baffled by the enigmatic four-thousand-year-old text.

The stories of ancient flying objects were no longer mere tales; they were pieces of history awaiting resolution, seemingly becoming almost tangible in his mind.

Rohan went to the archaeological site in Godawaya. Despite hours of searching underwater, the missing metal pieces eluded him. It seemed likely that they had been scattered and lost in the vast ocean over time. Ideally, he would have preferred to continue searching in the Indian Ocean, even if it took months or years. However, he understood that the archaeological department wouldn't fund such an expensive effort with only a slim chance of finding anything significant in the vastness of the ocean. Rohan returned to the shore, accepting the limitations of the situation.

Having changed out of his diving clothes and into a casual outfit, he gathered his belongings and prepared to leave. The shore remained tranquil, with only fisherfolk pulling in their nets as the tide receded. Just then, he spotted the seer again—the dusky woman with eyes that held the restlessness of a fighter.

This time, the woman's head was veiled by a thin, transparent cloth that allowed her hair to peek through. She approached him with concern, asking, "You're still here despite my warning? Aren't you afraid for your life?"

"I must complete my work before I leave," Rohan replied, focussing on packing his clothes into a sports bag.

"Is money more important to you than your very existence?"

"I've never really thought about it that way." Rohan paused. "But it's true that life can be challenging without money."

"Without life, you cannot exist," she argued.

"True, but the same goes for everyone, including you," he retorted.

"You don't know me.".

"Is that so? Are you saying you can live without life?"

"Well, I can tell you that one of my ancestors does."

"Who is that? Do I know her?"

"Everybody knows him," she replied cryptically.

"What's his name?"

"He's the powerful Asura, Ravana, with ten heads," she revealed.

"Is he alive? Tell me about the Asura."

"Now that you've decided to stay, you'll find out soon enough."

"You talk in riddles," Rohan remarked.

"Well, don't seers usually speak cryptic?"

"What's your name?"

"I am the seer for you."

"Tell me about my future. What does it look like?"

"Pain. Lots of agony. Loneliness. You will grieve. Your future depends on your today's actions. Act carefully."

"I don't need a seer to tell me that."

"Soon, things are going to change. You are just a mere mortal; you cannot alter fate. You don't take my words seriously, do you?

Time will tell—it's just a matter of time." With that, she walked away.

Rohan's mind swirled with countless questions, but the woman had already vanished into the forest. He stood there, trying to process the unsettling words she had spoken. Suddenly, like a bolt of lightning, her message struck him with force. "You are just a mortal. You cannot change what fate has decided for you," her words echoed in his mind. Was she not mortal? Who was she? Did she really possess knowledge about his future?

Determined to find out more, Rohan followed the woman into the nearby forest. He walked quickly, his heart pounding in his chest as he tried to keep up with the woman's swift pace. He saw her standing in the middle of the forest.

"What did you mean back there?" he asked.

The woman turned to face him; her eyes intense. "I have powers beyond your imagination," she answered. "Powers that you can only dream about."

He stood there, trying to understand what he had just heard. Powers beyond imagination. What could that mean? Could she potentially pose a threat to him? This was a question that required an answer. He forged ahead, tracing her footsteps and staying poised for any challenges.

Within the deserted forest, his surroundings transformed. The trees ascended to greater heights, reaching a monumental scale. The branches seemed to shift and move as if he had crossed into an entirely distinct realm. The twilight sky shifted in colour. The sun glowed with an otherworldly light.

Positioned behind the colossal tree, her elusive figure emerged in the distance. Her movements radiated an enchanting grace that was uniquely hers. She turned and looked directly at Rohan, her eyes seeming to glow. He could feel his heart pounding in his chest, unsure of what was about to happen next. The surface of the forest seemed to ripple and shift beneath her touch. Whatever lay beyond, he was ready to face it.

At first, it was just a flicker of movement, like a ripple in a pond, but then her body began to contort and twist. Her limbs elongated and shrank, her skin rippled and shifted, and her clothes seemed to stretch and change with her. Her transformation was incredible to behold. Her face turned, and her features grew more pronounced, her hair lengthening and changing colour before his eyes.

Her body became that of another woman, sleek and powerful, with piercing eyes glinted in the darkness. Rohan stood there, frozen, as she circled him, her eyes fixed on his, her face only half visible. He felt a sudden rush of fear.

Then, just as quickly as she had appeared, the half-faced woman began to shift again. Her body twisted and contorted once more; the half-face woman had become the seer again. Without a word, she turned and walked away. As he watched her disappear into the night, he knew the woman was not ordinary.

Unable to believe what he had just witnessed, he walked back, tracing the path he had taken until he reached the sandy beach. Watching a sudden and seemingly impossible transformation was a jarring experience. He questioned his own perception and wondered if what he had seen had been real or just a trick of the mind. A sense of danger took over him.

Having witnessed the woman transform into someone else, he felt threatened. He did not understand what was going on. However, the archaeologist in him felt a sense of curiosity, a fascination. Witnessing something so extraordinary and outside normal triggered his curiosity and amazement.

Despite the fear, his mind stayed on her and her ability to transform—a woman who could change her form. How could she have that extraordinary power? He should be careful when he meets her again. With a blend of exhaustion and elation, he was on a quest to know more about her, who she was and how she was related to the flying machine.

Rohan sat in the car with his head resting on the back of the seat. He closed his eyes while the driver steered the vehicle back to the hotel. Immersed in a gentle golden light that fell on him, every little detail of the seer and the half-faced woman remained engraved on his mind. Some danger was present, but he could not perceive it.

It was clear to him that she was not just a seer but something more than that. Suddenly, he remembered Professor Shastry's writing about the half-faced woman. It must be her, Kali, he thought. There were still many things to find out and untangle their secret. His mind drifted away.

It would be rather amusing if a time machine could take him back to be among the ancient South Asians, across the silence of four thousand years or more.

When Rohan returned to the hotel, it was quite dark. In his room, the balcony opened onto the mountains and valleys. He felt wrapped by a sense of warmth and noiselessness. Mira was busily typing on her laptop, papers scattered around her.

"You wouldn't believe what I saw today!" Rohan exclaimed to Mira.

"What did you see?" she asked, immersed in her writing.

"I don't think you'll believe me," Rohan hesitated.

"Come on, give it a try," Mira encouraged him.

With a mix of excitement and uncertainty, he proceeded to recount his extraordinary experience in the forest.

Chapter 8
The Copper Plates

Forget not all the words I say,
Nor let the occasion slip away.
Lo, with two spells I thee invest,
The mighty and the mightiest.
O'er thee fatigue shall ne'er prevail,
Nor age or change thy limbs assail.

—Valmiki Ramayana, Book I, Canto XXIV

The following morning, Rohan brought Mira along to the laboratory. Upon arrival, he introduced Mira to Priya.

"Professor Shastry was such an inspiration in my life. It's heartbreaking that he's gone. I'm so sorry for your loss," Priya said, offering Mira a friendly handshake.

"Oh, it's terrible!" Mira's face turned pale. "I can't believe how cruelly he was killed. I hope Inspector Chris will bring him justice. My father had sent me these photographs just before he died, and I was hoping you could help shed some light on them."

"Have you informed Inspector Chris about this?" Priya asked.

"Not yet," Mira replied.

"I believe you should tell him. He should be here soon. These are the photographs of the copper plates my husband bought in Berlin, which he later gave to the professor. Wait a minute." Priya walked away briefly and returned with more photographs in her hand. "Take a look at these. They are the same set of photographs taken by my husband." She placed them on the table for Mira to see.

"If only I could read them. I wonder what's inscribed on these plates," Mira remarked as she held the photographs. "Do you know where these copper plates are, Priya?"

"No, I don't. But I know a Sinhala script expert who could decipher them," Priya replied.

"That would be great, Priya," Rohan chimed in. "My mind is completely focused on this case; we must learn about it all we can."

"I have this feeling," Priya said nervously, "that very soon, I am going to meet my husband's murderer, and I am not ready for this."

"A dangerous man," Rohan remarked.

"How do you know it's a male?" Mira asked.

"I don't know. I'm guessing."

"There's one curious little question," Priya pointed out. "Is our archaeological investigation on the flying machine related to the two murder cases—one, my husband and two, Professor Shastry?"

"What do you make of this, Rohan?" Mira asked.

"The plot has thickened, but there's still much we don't know," Rohan replied.

"Maybe it's just an incredible coincidence," Mira suggested.

"A coincidence!" Priya exclaimed. "Two men were murdered in Lanka—both connected to history, both in possession of the same copper plates, and both linked to Ravana. They met a violent end. The odds are against this being a mere coincidence. Even our archaeological department and its activities are tied to this somehow, but I can't figure out the link."

"We need to tell the police everything we know," Mira said, growing restless.

"I hope I'm not interrupting," Inspector Chris said as he walked into the laboratory.

"Not at all," Rohan replied.

Inspector Chris was fascinated as he looked at the flying machine carefully assembled and displayed in the hall. "This is truly interesting! I've heard so much about it lately, even in the newspapers. They say flying machines were constructed in South Asia long before the Warner Brothers' time."

"We've made an important discovery in the murder case. Look at this," Rohan said, pointing towards the photographs.

"Where did you find them?" Chris inquired.

"My father, Professor Shastry, emailed them to me before he passed away," Mira explained.

"We have discovered the exact copper plates at the Island Hermitage where Professor Shastry used to reside," Chris added.

"You have found them. Where are they now?" Priya asked the inspector.

"They are safe in police custody. Once we've solved the case, we'll hand them over to the archaeological department."

"That's great news. We are planning to decipher the script on the copper plates," Priya said. "With the help of these photographs, our Sinhala expert might proceed, although he may need to examine the original plates in person if any doubts arise."

"Your Sinhala expert can come to our office. I'll instruct our department accordingly," Chris assured her.

"Do you have any idea who the murderer could be, Inspector?" Mira inquired.

"This case is incredibly complex, madam. Out of all the cases I've solved in my career, this one is the most challenging." the inspector explained. "We can't seem to obtain a list of strangers in the neighbourhood of Galle during the crime. The residents haven't been able to provide any evidence, and our attempts to find individuals who crossed the lake on the fateful day have been unsuccessful. So far, there have been no reports of mysterious or suspicious activities, and we haven't come across any unusual boat that might have landed in the lagoon through a water route."

"He might have travelled by air," Rohan remarked.

"That could be a possibility." The inspector smiled. "Besides, some peculiar elements have come to light in this case. The rope used to tie the victim's arms and legs appears to be something readily available in any hardware store. Unfortunately, no dealer in Galle seems to offer anything that could give us any clue about the identity of the murderer."

"Perhaps they are unwilling to give any clues," Rohan said thoughtfully. "Maybe they want to avoid being in the limelight."

"That could very well be the case," Chris replied. "It's as if the person responsible has vanished without a trace. The fact that there's a link between the two murders not only complicates the case but also worries me. What could have been the motive behind these killings? Perhaps the murderer is a lunatic with no clear motivation at all."

"I don't think you've analysed all the elements of the crime, Inspector," Rohan argued. "The only association that comes to my mind is the centuries-old folklore—the story of the famous king Ravana."

"Ha! That's an interesting idea." The inspector chuckled. "Ravana, the ten-headed Asura."

"We could be dealing with a superstition-crazed murderer," Rohan asserted.

"I thought," Chris said, "this whole thing to be a fairy tale. But considering Professor Shastry's research on the famous king Ravana, we can't simply dismiss it. If it holds some truth—"

"What's the connection between the discovery of the flying machine and Ravana?" Mira asked, cutting in.

"I can't recall the exact author of the article I read, but it discussed Ravana. It seems that Ravana's story has remained ingrained in people's minds for thousands of years," Priya explained.

"Perhaps," the inspector looked puzzled, "but who would benefit from murdering in the name of Ravana?"

"It could be a jealous writer, someone who couldn't succeed in the literary world," Mira suggested.

"Good lord!" Priya exclaimed. "I feel we might be on the right track now."

Chris stared at her momentarily and then let out a long, derisive chuckle. "You are probably right," he said.

Chapter 9
Deciphering

> Well-matched in size, strength, and skill
> They fought the dubious battle still.
> While sweat and blood, their limbs bedewed
> They met, retreated, and pursued:
>
> —Valmiki Ramayana, Book VI, Canto XL

The hall had a calm, reflective atmosphere, with soft lighting and minimal distractions. About fifty attendees filled the room—journalists, media personnel, university faculty, and research scholars—all eager to capture the moment, either in notes or through their cameras. They were waiting for Karthigesu's presentation on the copper plate inscriptions.

Priya shared the news of Mohana Bandara's arrival. He was the director of the archaeological department of Lanka, a prestigious position. Though in his early seventies, he looked surprisingly youthful. Dressed casually in jeans and a cotton shirt, he sported perfectly parted hair. His smile revealed an almost unreal set of impeccably white teeth.

"Good afternoon," Bandara greeted. Priya introduced Mira, Inspector Chris, and Rohan. "I am deeply sorry about your father, Professor Shastry," Bandara said to Mira. "Although I had met him only once, I am a staunch follower of his work and ideas. His death is a great loss."

"Thank you for your kind words," Mira replied.

Bandara turned his attention to Rohan, and they discussed his underwater exploration and field archaeology work. He praised

Rohan's excellence in the field and expressed high hopes for his work in Lanka.

"Ah, Professor Karthigesu. We've been looking forward to your arrival," Priya said, introducing him as a linguist specialising in the Sinhala script.

Karthigesu began his presentation by delving into the copper plate inscriptions and revealing that the original text likely originated from Lanka. The inscriptions mentioned a Buddhist monk who safeguarded the chronicles. His long beard gently brushed his chest as he spoke, adding an air of wisdom to his presence.

"For convenience, I've categorised the collection of copper plates into sections based on the subject matter of the inscriptions. They unveil a fascinating series of legends." Karthigesu paused to clean his glasses with his T-shirt. Shielding his eyes from the sunlight streaming through the window, he resumed his presentation:

"The copper plates were unfortunately fragmented and in poor condition. After weeks of painstaking effort, I assembled as much as possible, recovering approximately seventy-five per cent of the inscriptions. Originally, there were ten plates, all contributing to one story, and I successfully restored substantial portions of it."

"Do you have any specific dates for the plates?" Someone in the audience asked Karthigesu.

"Carbon analysis places it around the first century BCE, and the language of the inscription matches that era. It's written in Sinhala Prakrit," Karthigesu explained.

Then, he paused, brushing his beard thoughtfully as his eyes scanned the papers.

"I've only managed to gather fragments of it. The text itself claims to belong to the time of King Ravana but was written down much later. Unravelling the ancient words has been a painstaking task, revealing a seven-thousand-year-old story of a king,"

Mira eagerly scribbled Karthigesu's words in her notebook while Rohan and Inspector Chris listened to his captivating explanation.

"The city of Lanka, built by Ravana, was among the world's most ancient cities," Karthigesu continued. "The copper plates narrate Ravana's marriage with Mandodari. Mahamuni Maya, chief architect of the ancient world, played a significant role in their wedding.

"He gifted Ravana a flying machine, designed and built by him, with a circumference of twenty-four Hastas and equipped with four wheels. The Hastas, an ancient unit of measurement, is approximately eighty-three centimetres."

Pausing briefly to refer to his papers, Karthigesu continued, "Ravana's empire flourished before the Great War against Rama, and Wariyapola in the north-western province of Lanka served as his airport. The text also portrays Ravana's domination over other kingdoms."

"Ravana's flying machine was a marvel of engineering and technology well ahead of its time. When he abducted Sita and took her to Lanka, he did so in his flying ship, equipped with various weapons and defences for protection."

He further shared the fascinating tale of Jatayu, a mighty man capable of transforming into an eagle. While exploring different lands, Jatayu witnessed Ravana's abduction of Sita and followed them in his eagle form. In an attempt to rescue Sita, Jatayu courageously confronted Ravana, encountering not only his strength and magic but also the advanced techniques of the flying machine. The ensuing battle left Jatayu mortally wounded, providing further evidence of Ravana's possession of the flying machine.

During Karthigesu's presentation, Rohan's attention briefly shifted towards the audience. As he scanned the room, he spotted a familiar face—the seer. Wearing a journalist badge on her blouse, she appeared engrossed in her work, diligently jotting down notes like the other journalists.

Rohan remained vigilant, scrutinising her for any signs of hidden motives. Turning to a journalist beside him, he gestured toward the seer and asked who she was.

"Uru? She works for the Daily Mirror," the journalist replied.

Rohan silently repeated her name, his gaze fixed on her, searching for any sign of her intentions. At that moment, two men with elaborate hair knots entered the hall and sat beside Uru. They appeared like bodyguards assigned to protect her. One of the men leaned in and whispered something into her ears. Suddenly, Uru rose from her seat, displaying an expression that hinted at anger, and swiftly left the hall.

Uru's sudden departure with her bodyguards left Rohan intensely curious. Questions swirled in his mind about her true identity, her role as a journalist, and whether a hidden agenda lay behind her appearance. Did her bodyguard's whispered words provoke anger, or was something else at play?

Memories of their earlier encounter resurfaced, reminding him of the seer's warning, the uncanny transformation he had witnessed, and the subsequent events that followed. His mind raced, searching for clues and seeking answers to the mysteries surrounding Uru. The thought that she might be concealing her true intentions only fuelled Rohan's mistrust and reinforced the need for caution.

Rohan's attention went back to Karthigesu's words, sensing

that a revelation connecting the present with a fragment of the past was about to unfold. The remarkable inscription Karthigesu shared seemed to emerge from the shadows, shedding light on a long-forgotten history. "Here's another fascinating tale described in this inscription, presented clearly for all to read. It begins with a magical forest hidden deep in the heart of India, where a group of Asuras resided. They took on the role of guardians, fiercely protecting the plants, animals, and creatures dwelling within the forest.

"All these accounts and a considerable part of folklore lead me to believe this country is a significant cradle of Asian civilisation. Alongside the Indian subcontinent, it is the birthplace of languages, arts, and science. Its literature holds precious records of antiquity.

"Although these inscriptions may not directly relate to the ancient flying machine or the manuscript, they still take us to a different level of understanding," Karthigesu concluded.

Priya and Karthigesu walked together to the car park. He seemed hesitant as if grappling with whether to share something.

"I hope I was of some help," Karthigesu said.

"You were fantastic," Priya replied, gently patting his back. "I am truly impressed. This could be a ground-breaking reconstruction of South Asia's history."

"It wasn't easy at all. I dedicated days and nights to it. I'll provide you with everything I have—photographs of the copper plates, the original Sinhala version, its English translation, a chronological account, and a summary. I'll prepare a professional report within two days."

He hesitated for a moment before speaking again. "There is something I can't quite put into words right now. It's as if there's more to this story than meets the eye. I need some time to sort through my thoughts."

"What is it, Karthigesu? Tell me," she insisted.

"I received a death warning with some advice to stop my work, but I'm not sure which aspect of my work it's referring to," Karthigesu shared. "Is it my twenty-year-long teaching job, my writing on ancient Lankan languages and cultural influences, or my deciphering of the copper plates?"

"Who sent you these warnings?" Priya inquired.

"I have no idea. I found a letter in my mailbox with no name or sender information."

"You should talk to Inspector Chris about this," Priya suggested.

"Today, I received a second letter urging me to immediately stop my work and refrain from speaking to anyone about it. I can't gauge how serious these warnings are. It might just be a prank, but what if someone is trying to intimidate me? These students at the university can be quite unpredictable."

"You should inform the police about these threats." Priya insisted.

"How is your husband?" Karthigesu asked casually.

"He is dead. You didn't know?"

"No, I'm so sorry,"

"How are you? And your wife?"

"I never married. The girl I loved was in love with someone else."

"Sorry about that," she said.

Priya was the girl Karthigesu had loved during their college days. He still found her attractive and wanted to gather his thoughts before speaking further. He sensed the risk and decided to remain guarded in his own words. Above all else, he needed to focus on the message and the messenger.

"I need to go and finish my work for today," he said clumsily, uncertain what else to say.

As he started his car, she suggested, "Maybe we should go out for dinner to renew our college days. This weekend?"

"This weekend," he agreed.

Chapter 10
The Linguist

> Then tell me all, thou holy Sage,
> And whose this pleasant hermitage
> In which those wicked one's delight
> To mar and kill each holy rite.
> And with foul heart and evil deed
> Thy sacrifice, great Saint, impede.

—Valmiki Ramayana, Book I, Canto XXX

The following morning, Rohan sat in the car and instructed the driver to take him to Badulla. As they started off leaving the resort, he discreetly caught a glimpse of Uru, the seer. With her, he noticed the presence of the men he had seen before when Karthigesu presented the copper plates. Both of them were walking together towards the resort.

Rohan asked the driver to stop the car, and once it came to a halt, he requested the driver to wait while he went to the main gate of the resort, situated at the slightly curved end of the road. Uru and her companions were no longer in sight as if they had vanished. He searched the surroundings, but there was no sign of them. Rohan presumed they must have slipped into the nearby forest across the road. Feeling puzzled, he returned to the car.

"Is everything all right, sir?" the driver asked Rohan.

"Did you see anyone at the gate?"

"No, sir. I saw no one."

"There were three people—two men and a woman. She had long hair tied up on their crown," Rohan explained.

"I am sorry, sir, I must've been concentrating on driving."

"By the way, do you know any native Lankans? Indigenous people, the original inhabitants of this island."

The driver began to share his knowledge about the Asuras, referring to them as the fire people, forest dwellers and tribal groups who had lived in the area for generations. According to popular belief, they possessed supernatural powers and were known to be unkind and dangerous, with great strength and magical abilities.

It was said that Asuras could disguise themselves, making it impossible for anyone to recognise them. Despite their fearsome reputation, some Asuras were considered kind and protectors of the natural world, while others were known to be mischievous yet caring people.

After a while, the driver parked the car at the archaeologist's office in Badulla. A uniformed man stood at the door. Inside, Rohan noticed Priya engaged in conversation with Inspector Chris.

Inspector Chris seemed to speak cautiously, continually nodding his head. Still, it was unclear to Rohan whether it was a professional habit meant to display confidence or part of a facade to pretend he knew everything happening. He revealed that Professor Karthigesu, who had visited them the previous day to decipher the copper plates, was found dead in his car with a broken neck. A passer-by had discovered his body. The forensic examination yielded troubling findings, but they couldn't definitively determine whether he was killed or if it was an accident.

"What do you mean, Inspector?" Rohan couldn't believe what he had just heard.

Priya stood there, unable to find the right words after hearing the distressing news.

"There is a probability," Inspector Chris continued, "and I stress on the word probability that a blow from a solid object caused the fracture at the base of the skull. However, no object inside the car could have caused such a head injury."

Rohan leaned on the table, trying to grasp the situation.

"I only mention that as a probability. The initial inspection and autopsy seem to point towards death caused by an accident, as the car has small dents," Chris responded.

"What are you trying to say?" Priya sounded restless.

"I'm trying to share the facts without delving too much into technical details. There are certain aspects, like the type of fracture and the position of the body, which have raised reasonable doubts," Inspector Chris replied.

"That's terrible!" Priya said, baffled.

Chris nodded in agreement and continued, "A blow to the back of the neck could have been fatal for Professor Karthigesu. It's possible that someone then placed him in the driver's seat and intentionally bumped the car from the back to create the appearance of an accident. We are currently conducting a forensic study to investigate the possibility that the killer struck him twice, not just once—a first blow to incapacitate him and a second to ensure his death."

"And there's another crucial point," Chris added. "We found burnt papers a few metres away from the accident. The surviving fragments revealed that they were photographs of archaeological objects and related documents. It appears that someone intentionally set fire to the papers that were inside the car. Among the fragments, we found some with Karthigesu's name, which led us to conclude that they belonged to the victim."

Priya looked at Rohan, seemingly unable to process what she had just heard. The news of Karthigesu's death and the loss of his valuable work left her baffled. "I am shocked beyond words," she said. "I can't believe that Karthigesu, whom we met just yesterday, is now dead, and all his hard work is gone forever."

"Let's assume for a moment that his death wasn't an accident. Do you have any suspicions who might have wanted to harm him?" Rohan inquired.

"I have no idea. That's why I'm relying on your help to solve this case," Chris admitted.

"How can we help you, Inspector?" Rohan asked.

Inspector Chris's manner changed, and he looked at Priya with a methodical sluggishness. His friendliness seemed to vanish as he posed a question that felt like a coarse demand, almost trying to create a doubtful conspiracy between them. "You've known Karthigesu for a long time, haven't you? Forgive me, but murder is a cruel business," he said, a disturbing smile creeping onto his face. "You knew him from your college days, is that correct?"

"Yes, that's correct."

"And you were in love," Chris then claimed.

"What? That's not true," Priya responded, startled.

Chris added, "We found a letter in his room addressed to you. He expresses his love for you, dating back to his college days."

"I have never received any letter from him," Priya said agitatedly.

Inspector Chris had managed to uncover a significant aspect of Priya's life, delving into a sensitive area where the wounds from her husband's death were still fresh, and now, she was faced with the loss of an old friend who had never expressed his true feelings to her. As Chris calculated his next steps, Priya couldn't help but worry about her reputation. The murder case was shrouded in mystery, leaving them with too many unknowns. She prepared to defend herself.

However, Inspector Chris didn't display kindness or sympathy; his approach was purely based on law enforcement tactics. He focused on doing his job, attempting to view the situation from a legal perspective. The only lead he had at that moment was the revelation of Karthigesu's secret girlfriend. According to Priya, Karthigesu had never confessed his love to her.

"Even if he had such feelings for me, that's history. After college, I never saw him. It's only now, after years." She managed to hide her surprise, though her expression indicated she found Chris's comment reckless. "There was nothing between Karthigesu and me."

"You were here when Karthigesu presented his translation of the text from the copper plates," Rohan added, "Priya had merely asked for his help to decipher the text, and that was the extent of their interaction. He left after presenting his work. But before we continue, I want to know whether Karthigesu's death was an accident or not."

"I don't have any conclusive evidence," Chris replied.

"If you suspect Karthigesu's death and you're trying to extract information from us, I want to know right away if we're being interrogated as suspects. If that's the case, we'll need to talk to our lawyers," Rohan said.

"That won't be necessary," Chris reassured. "The current official report states that Professor Karthigesu died in an accident."

"But what if the forensic investigators change their report?" Rohan said, raising a concern.

"In that situation, you and others who knew the victim will be considered potential suspects. The list could be extensive, especially considering his university connections—suspended students, jealous colleagues, and more. However, your statement will be valuable, given that you met him before his death," Chris explained.

"Professor Karthigesu mentioned that he had received anonymous death-warning letters," Priya recalled. "He said he received them at least twice and had no idea who sent them. He believed it might have been a prank from one of his students."

"Yes, we found such letters in his house," Chris confirmed, "but they were electronic printouts and offered no significant leads. This case is quite unusual."

"I'm completely perplexed," Priya expressed, "I don't understand who could have killed Professor Karthigesu and why."

"That is an excellent question." Chris took a sip from his alcohol flask and walked away.

Rohan watched Inspector Chris and the uniformed man return to their car. He observed Priya, who seemed worried.

That evening in the hotel room, a gentle glow emanated from the table lamp as Rohan switched on some jazz music. He sat on the terrace with Mira beside him. Reclining in a chair, he had a glass of wine in his hand. The music filled his mind, and the wine eased down his throat, yet an inexplicable sense of unease and foreboding lingered.

Rohan took a deep breath, realising that too many people he knew had already passed away. He found himself gazing up at the night sky, the moon and the stars surrounded by darkness as the tropical wind rustled through the rolling hills. The forest enveloped them with an air of mystery, accompanied by the warm scent of nearby tea plantations and wildflowers. Rohan found it challenging to grasp the true nature of reality as if something sinister was hidden behind the scenes. He became more alert for any signs of danger.

Meanwhile, Mira diligently worked on her father's unfinished book, immersing herself in writing, rewriting, and editing. Influenced by her late father, Professor Shastry, she felt compelled to complete his book.

Rohan informed Mira about the news of Professor Karthigesu's death, explaining that Inspector Chris was merely speculating about it possibly being a murder. He rationalised that accidents on the road were common and reckless driving could lead to fatalities.

Mira was shocked and alarmed by the possible killing of Professor Karthigesu. Considering his recent work deciphering the copper plates, she wondered who could bear ill feelings towards him. She couldn't shake off the fear that her father's, Priya's husband's, and now Karthigesu's deaths were somehow connected.

Rohan expressed his concern for Mira's safety, advising her to be careful. She worried about him, but Rohan assured her he would remain vigilant. He urged her to stay within the resort and not venture out alone, to which Mira promised she would adhere.

That night, Rohan felt an uncomfortable sensation, an overwhelming presence of danger. It was as though something was in the air, disturbing his peace of mind. He couldn't put a finger on it, wondering if it was merely his imagination. Unknown to him, someone was lurking in the shadows, under the shade of a tree, observing, listening to their music, and scrutinising every move they made.

Chapter 11
The Model

Those robbed at such a time obtain
Their plundered store and wealth again.
He, like a fish that takes the bait,
In the briefest time, he shall meet his fate.
—Valmiki Ramayana, Book III, Canto LXIX

Aeronautical engineer Sunil De Silva shook the rain off his hair, standing awkwardly in the lobby as water dripped from his soaked clothes, pooling around his feet. His trousers clung to his legs, and he looked unmistakably out of place. A sizeable object rested in his hand, and he seemed unsure where to place it in the archaeologist's office.

"Have you managed to solve it?" Priya inquired, closing the door behind him.

"Sort of," he responded, hesitatingly handing the object to Priya and following her into the laboratory.

"What's the problem?" She asked.

Sunil seemed more focused on how to act in the unfamiliar setting than showing interest in his surroundings.

"Well, there isn't a problem," he explained. "It's just a matter of dedicating time and thought to it. These days, I only think about the ancient flying object." Sunil unwrapped the model from its plastic cover with great fascination and placed it carefully on the floor. His expression shifted from elusive to intensely captivated, revealing his unwavering dedication to solving the mystery behind the artefact.

Priya couldn't help but notice that he wasn't exaggerating when he claimed that the flying machine consumed his every thought; he was determined to solve its complexity.

"It looks fabulous," Rohan remarked, drawn closer to the artefact.

"I reconstructed the model based on the artefact, but it wasn't without its challenges. Since I couldn't determine the composition of the unknown alloy, I decided to use aluminium, which I could easily access in my lab. I had to be cautious about the weight to match your artefact's specifications.

"It's an interesting type of aircraft, exhibiting characteristics of both helicopters and conventional planes, yet lacking the sturdiness and stability of the latter. Additionally, due to the missing front part, I had to imagine its possible design.

"Since we have no clues about its original engine, I used components from my old rotorcraft as a reference. I employed an unpowered autorotation mechanism for lift, similar to helicopters, and an engine-powered propeller, like that of a fixed-wing aircraft, to generate thrust. What we have here is a conventional model of an aircraft."

"Can this thing fly?" Rohan inquired.

Sunil offered a slight nod, seemingly hesitant to make any definitive claims. "It all boils down to physics. If you have experience in modelling, you'll see things from a different perspective. Aircraft are incredibly sensitive to even the tiniest design mistakes. A minor error can make it challenging to control or prevent it from taking off.

"The build needs to be strong and precise, adhering to the laws of physics. The landing gear, especially the tail-wheel assembly, must be excellent. This includes the wheels, as they endure significant loads during take-off. If the aircraft can't handle the load well, it may wobble or bend, making take-offs difficult or impossible."

"To ensure a smooth flight," he continued, "I finished the blades using an electronic scale with 0.1-gram precision. Thankfully, I had a remote-controlled engine to construct this model. Allow me to demonstrate how she flies."

Sunil pulled a remote controller from his bag and pressed a green button. The model took off into the air with a buzzing sound. A faint twitch at one corner of Sunil's mouth was a polite reflex. The gleam in his eyes grew brighter, showcasing his fascination with his creation.

"I must say, not bad," Sunil approved. "We must remember that what we've constructed is merely a possibility. In ancient times, reality might have been quite different. We've taken the crucial first step by building a flying machine that resembles the artefact."

"Sunil, how would you describe the person behind this creation?" Rohan asked.

"Well, it's difficult to say. Someone who had a thorough understanding of engineering and design principles. A highly talented individual, an expert in metallurgy, skilled in angles and symmetry, who surely enjoyed building it." His eyes showed admiration, like a scientist's instinctive respect for another. He pulled the book Vaimanika Shastra from his bag and placed it on the table. "This book contains false information," he asserted.

"So, you mean the entire book is a fake," Rohan said, puzzled.

Sunil gestured evasively, trying not to draw any definitive conclusions. "I'm not making any strong claims. I'm just considering the possibility that the author might have used the fake manuscript as a diversion to protect the authenticity of the original artefact," he explained, flipping through a few pages of the book. Then, he pointed to a specific description of creating a *Pinjulaa* mirror. "Take a look at this," he said. "I tried to follow this description and ended up with a useless mess. To confirm my suspicions, I contacted a friend working at the Indian Institute of Science, who had also tried to build a flying machine using this book. He confirmed that the description was fake.

"If you examine the flying machine described in this book," Sunil said, flipping to the pages, "you'll notice that they lack any real engineering substance. They appear more like poorly constructed fabrications than a flying machine's functional specifications. The descriptions and illustrations don't align thematically or technically. While the language and content suggest an ancient origin, the text is incomplete, ambiguous, and filled with errors."

"Sunil, I'm impressed," Rohan praised, shaking his hand and giving him a friendly pat. "You've done splendid work. But why would a celebrated scholar like Pundit Subbaraya Shastry create a manuscript with fake instructions?"

"It doesn't seem like a coincidence," Sunil replied. "The way this manuscript is written, it was deliberately created by someone familiar with terms and details of mechanical engineering."

"I must admit, I fell into the trap of believing the manuscript was authentic," Priya said.

"This leads us in a different direction that somewhere in the world, there exists an original version of the Vaimanika Shastra, the aeronautical science," Rohan said, glancing at Priya.

"I have to leave now," Sunil said. "There's an important meeting I must attend. If you need me, give me a call."

"Thank you, Sunil!" Rohan called out, ensuring his departing colleague heard his appreciation.

Sunil waved his arm in acknowledgement before closing the door behind him.

"Rohan, I want to show you something," Priya said, leading the way out of the hall and into the storeroom, with Rohan following closely.

Priya held in her hand a remarkable ancient coffer with intricate designs. The coffer was small in breadth, long, and slim, made of yellow metal adorned with beautiful carvings that had lost its shine due to age.

Rohan took it from her, examining the exquisite piece. He noticed it was empty. "I've seen a similar one before, he said. "There must have been a manuscript inside."

"As per the records," she said, "the coffer was found on the top layers during excavation, but it was unearthed empty. We haven't found any manuscript associated with it to this day. Egon von Eickstedt might have taken it. He was a German anthropologist who came to Lanka in 1920 for anthropological studies. It's known that he took artefacts with him."

Rohan's passion lies in exploring artefacts beyond their mere factual aspects. He was searching for a clue, a recipe to unite different stories floating like dead leaves on the dark water of time.

Chapter 12
The Director

> Bristled in dread, each starting hair
> As Shiva strove with Vishnu there.
> But Vishnu raised his voice again.
> And Shiva's bowstring twanged in vain.
> Its master of the Three bright Eyes
> Stood fixt in fury and surprise.
>
> —Valmiki Ramayana, Book I, Canto LXXV

Sitting across from Priya and Rohan was Mohana Bandara, the director of the archaeological department. He asked for a cup of coffee, made himself comfortable and brought up the sad news about Professor Karthigesu's passing. "Professor Karthigesu's untimely death seems like someone has an ugly motivation."

Priya expressed her disbelief over Karthigesu's sad demise, questioning whether it was an accident. If not, she wondered who could have killed him and what motive might lie behind such an act. She expressed her optimism that Inspector Chris would be able to uncover the truth promptly. As the conversation progressed, she brought up another point. "Adding to the unfolding situation," she said, "you mentioned that the ancient manuscript we believed to have in our inventory is missing."

Bandara took a deep breath before speaking. "My dear lady, our archaeological department takes its responsibilities seriously," he said.

"I do not doubt that, sir," Priya replied. "But our research on the coffer has revealed some crucial information that could potentially change the direction of our investigation."

The office clerk entered the room and gently placed three cups of coffee on the table.

"To understand the fate of the manuscript, it's important to grasp the historical context of the location. Let me explain," Bandara continued, "The Portuguese arrived in 1505, followed by Dutch and British explorers who later set foot on our island.

"The kingdom of Kandy, supported by the Asuras, stood as an independent monarchy. Discontent grew among the people against British rule, leading to a rebellion. The Uva Rebellion in 1817 marked a dark chapter. The British orchestrated a devastating massacre.

"Over time, this rebellion evolved into a prolonged guerrilla conflict against European powers. The British suppressed the rebels with mass killings as a grim warning to the rest of Lanka. Lanka transformed into British Ceylon, a Crown colony under British rule."

"Challenging times," Rohan acknowledged.

"Absolutely." The director nodded as if he had witnessed those events first-hand. "Back then, if you weren't aligned with the British, you were essentially against them. The Asuras bore the brunt of this conflict, losing their cherished freedom. In response, they concealed the flying machine and the manuscript, keeping them hidden from the British.

"Some years ago, I discovered a remarkable discovery while studying archaeological records. It came to my attention that German anthropologist Egon von Eickstedt led a major expedition to this island.

"His initial visit to Badulla was in 1920. He travelled across Asia, focusing on racial research. During his time in Badulla, Eickstedt collected artefacts. The Asuras struck a deal with Hitler, offering Eickstedt the manuscript in exchange for his assistance overthrowing the British and restoring their freedom in Lanka. Eickstedt returned to Germany. Recently, I couldn't resist the urge to go to Germany myself."

"Why didn't you bring them back to Lanka?" Rohan inquired, pushing for more details.

"This, I couldn't achieve. The Germans compelled me to sign a contract on behalf of the archaeological department. They paid a respectable sum for those artefacts," the director explained.

"Did you come across the Vaimanika Shastra?" Rohan asked.

"Yes. I had the chance to see the original version," the elderly man replied, seemingly lost in his memories.

Towards the end of their conversation, Rohan noticed a solitary black crow perched on a nearby tree. The bird appeared unusually still as if listening to their conversation.

Its eyes held a weird hint of intelligence and understanding beyond an ordinary bird's. Then, almost like a dream, the crow began to transform. Its wings grew longer and thinner, its beak shrunk, and its feathers became more colourful and shining. Within moments, the crow had morphed into a beautiful woman with long, flowing hair and eyes glinted with otherworldly wisdom.

Perched upon the tree, the woman looked at Rohan with an intensity that seemed to gauge his worth. Before any words could escape Rohan's lips, she gracefully unfurled her wings, soaring into the sky and leaving a sense of awe and wonder behind. As the crow circled overhead, Rohan, unable to hold his astonishment, signalled the others, "Look at the bird!" All eyes followed his gesture, seeing the magnificent creature. "That's an Asura. I saw the bird transform into a woman." Rohan's voice filled with surprise.

Priya dismissed his account as a daydream, leaving Rohan with a puzzling question: why had no one else seen the spectacle he had just witnessed? How could such a remarkable sight have escaped everyone's notice?

Chapter 13
The Kidnap

> From her small foot, an anklet fair
> With jewels slipped and through the air,
> Like a bright circlet of the flame
> Of thunder, to the valley came.
>
> —Valmiki Ramayana, Book III, Canto LII

The resort where Mira and Rohan stayed looked like a castle, with its breathtaking view of the Ella Gap. Rohan made his way from the garden towards their room, raindrops gently falling on him. Upon entering the room, he noticed Mira's absence. His mind was a whirlwind of thoughts, ranging from Professor Karthigesu to Professor Shastry and his wife, Mira.

The question of her whereabouts echoed. He tried to reach her by phone, but his calls went unanswered. He walked over to the table where Mira usually worked. The table, typically scattered with handwritten notes and printouts, now stood empty.

While he was waiting anxiously for her return, Rohan stretched out on the sofa. Something unknown seemed to brood over him. Abruptly, he caught the sound of a cry. Mira's voice called out to him, piercing through the haze of drowsiness. Alert and responsive, he rose from the sofa. The room was dimmed, and he realised he had dozed off while still wearing his daytime clothes and shoes.

Glancing at his watch, he noted it was a quarter past midnight. Checking his phone, he found no response from Mira. He pulled open the window shutters and looked outside. Scary thoughts crossed his mind. He hurried downstairs to the reception.

"Have you seen my wife?" he asked the receptionist.

"No, sir. Is she not in your room?"

"No, she's not there." Rohan panicked. "Did anything out of the ordinary occur today?"

"Nothing, sir," the receptionist answered. "Have you checked the restaurant?"

"She's not there either," he replied tersely.

The resort manager extended his assistance in the search for Mira. They combed through the estate and garden, checking every nook and cranny. Returning to the room, they found everything seemingly undisturbed. Where could she be? After all, she had assured him she wouldn't venture out alone. In a state of growing anxiety, he made another attempt to call her, leaving an urgent message for her to call back.

When the manager opened the terrace door and summoned Rohan, he hurried over. The sight that met his eyes on the terrace caused a shiver to run down his spine. There, on the ground, lay Mira's laptop, shattered into pieces, accompanied by burnt papers.

Beyond the garden's boundaries, the land dropped sharply into a rocky precipice on the mountain range. They circumvented the wooden fence, searching for any sign of her, but the darkness hindered their efforts.

Rohan felt the weight of urgency pressing on him. He called Inspector Chris, who did not respond either. Leaving a voicemail, he urged Chris to come to the resort immediately, emphasising Mira's disappearance and his dire need for assistance.

The resort manager's inquiry about the last time Rohan had seen Mira tugged at his heartstrings, particularly the manager's phrasing, the *last time*. "This morning, before I headed to work,"

Rohan responded with a heavy sigh. The eastern horizon was beginning to reveal a faint orange line heralding the impending dawn. The wind brushed past Rohan. Occasionally, a bird darted through the garden, its call piercing the air.

The manager left, assuring Rohan of his willingness to assist in any way possible. Rohan expressed gratitude for the support, though he recognised there was little more he could do than wait in this uncertain situation.

In the early hours of the morning, Inspector Chris arrived. Rohan gave him a comprehensive overview of Mira's situation, recounting the laptop's destruction and the burnt papers discovered on the terrace. Chris's reaction was one of shock, seemingly caught off guard by the abruptness of the incident and the striking similarity to previous murder cases. As Chris surveyed the room, Rohan's sense of apprehension deepened.

"Forgive my delay; I came as soon as I received your message," Chris stated a notable shift in his tone. He had transformed somehow; his manner had grown more intense and solemn in response to the critical turn the case had taken. He meticulously examined the room with an odd blend of hope and concern in his gaze.

"Our priority is to locate her swiftly before something terrible happens to her," Chris admitted, his unease not fully concealed. "I understand your feelings. In past cases, the victim's remains were found alongside the charred papers. But we have reason to believe Mira is still alive. We must hold onto that hope."

Chris's words, coupled with the mention of Mira and the victim's body, stirred an unsettling fear within Rohan, causing his legs to weaken. Following sunrise, a team of police officers scoured the garden for evidence. The resort's staff were interrogated, and their knowledge of the situation was probed.

Inspector Chris asserted the gravity of the circumstances, insisting that no one could leave the resort without permission and that outsiders, apart from guests, were barred from entry.

A cry from one of the officers pierced the air, prompting Inspector Chris to rush towards the source of the call. "We've found something that might be significant," the officer reported, crouching down, indicating an object.

Rohan made his way to the location along with Chris. Two investigators focused on a specific spot on the lawn, one kneeling for closer examination. The kneeling investigator rose, a mobile phone held in his hand.

"That's Mira's!" Rohan said, his voice laced with concern.

"There are indications of a struggle here," Chris noted. "The disarray is evident, long trails on the soft ground like a struggle for balance. Here, steps veer down to the right. The struggle seems to have ended at this point. The footprints are more pronounced." Then, he addressed the other officers, "We need to carefully document and identify these footprints."

"Your wife displayed remarkable resilience, even in those challenging moments; she seemed to be leading us somewhere," Chris shared with Rohan. "It becomes clear why the struggle stopped. She must have realised the need to leave a trace behind, and that's when she likely cooperated quietly. The ground becomes firmer at this point, preventing her from leaving distinct footprints. She adopted an alternative strategy by discarding her ring here. Could you please confirm if this ring belongs to your wife?"

"Yes, this is Mira's ring. It's our wedding ring," Rohan replied.

"Your wife's resourcefulness is commendable," Chris said. "The markings she left continue, even beyond the fence. It's like two individuals dragging and one woman resisting, all indicating a path. Everyone, let's cross the fence and search for more clues."

"Please be careful, the area is hazardous," cautioned the resort manager, positioned near the fence alongside Rohan.

"More clues are present here. I've spotted an earring," Chris remarked. He hastened towards Rohan, earring in hand. "Does this belong to your wife?"

"Yes, it does," Rohan affirmed. Despite being held captive, she managed to discreetly remove her earrings—her hands evidently unbound. He studied the imprints on the ground left by her feet, distinctly identifying Mira's smaller footprints amidst the larger ones of her captors. He recalled reading Ravana's abduction of Sita and how she had dropped jewels as markers for Rama. Mira appeared to be employing a similar strategy.

"Your wife was taken away from that cliff," Chris revealed.

"Taken away? How can you be certain?" Rohan questioned.

"That cliff serves as an ideal landing and take-off site. Observe these anchor-like impressions—it's as though an airship had been secured here," Chris explained. "By scrutinising the cliff's edge, you'll notice marks here. Almost as if something lifted off into the air, leaving no tyre or wheel imprints. Given the absence of sound reported by anyone at the resort. I assume it was a flying machine."

Chapter 14
The Failed Rescue

Faint is his voice, and near to die,
He scarce can lift his trembling eye.
Jatáyu, if thou still can speak,
Give, give the answer that I seek.

—Valmiki Ramayana, Book III, Canto LXIX

It was nine in the morning. Rohan had not slept at all the previous night. He was desperate to hear some good news about Mira, but the waiting time was unbearably long. With each distressing notion that crossed his thoughts, he paced restlessly around the room, bracing himself to face the uncertainties of the world.

The sudden knock at the door jolted him from his thoughts, triggering a sense of alarm. He grappled with the decision to open it or not. The persistent knocking prompted him to approach cautiously. He leaned in and looked through the keyhole. A rush of relief washed over him as he spotted Priya standing on the other side. He unlatched the door, allowing her to step inside.

"Any news about Mira?" Priya inquired with concern.

"I was just about to ask you the same thing," he responded with a sigh.

"Unfortunately, our director, Mohana Bandara, was severely injured in a serious accident. He's currently in the intensive care unit at the local hospital, fighting for his life. Strangely enough, it appears that Mira's kidnappers were the ones who targeted him when he attempted to rescue her."

"I need to visit him immediately. Let's head to the hospital," he asserted.

The sun hung high in the sky, casting an intense glare that washed out the hues of the heavens and cast a subdued tone upon the palm trees. Inside the hospital room, Bandara lay on the bed, a bandage stained with blood adorning his chest. Engaged in a conversation with Inspector Chris, he recounted his experience while the inspector diligently recorded his words.

Bandara's gaze, weary yet determined, shifted towards Rohan, his hand raising slightly in a gesture of acknowledgement. Responding to the unspoken signal, Rohan approached his bedside.

"I'm truly sorry, Rohan. I couldn't rescue your wife," Bandara whispered,

"Who did this to you? And where did you see Mira?"

Struggling to find his strength, Bandara began to recount his harrowing tale, "Yesterday afternoon, around four o'clock, I was hiking in the central highlands, off the beaten path near Adam's Peak. Familiar with the terrain due to my frequent mountain climbing, I took a route that was less travelled.

"As I reached the summit, an unusual flying machine caught my attention. It descended and landed near a cave. Two figures emerged from the craft, dragging a woman with them. They forced her into the cave. It was your wife, Mira. I knew it immediately.

"One of the men tied her hands together to restrain her. She sat there, crying. My first thought was to call the police, but my phone battery had died. I felt an urgent need to act. Carefully, I made my way towards her, planning to free Mira and escape while her captors were distracted.

"As I started untying her, one of the men spotted me. He shot an arrow in my direction. These men were like warriors—I couldn't fight them. The arrow struck me, and I collapsed to the ground, helpless. Mira's cries echoed as they carried her away to the north.

"Wounded, bleeding, and alone, I lay there in the quiet of the forest, convinced I wouldn't survive. After what felt like an eternity, a passerby found me, helped me, and brought me to this hospital. I'm sorry, Rohan. I couldn't save Mira."

"You took a huge risk trying to save her," Rohan remarked. "I appreciate that. To know that Mira is alive offers some comfort. Who were those men who took Mira?"

"The Asuras. The flying machine, bamboos." Bandara struggled to talk, his breathing becoming laboured. "A trail of yellow in the sky," he managed to say before succumbing to coughs.

Priya hurried to get help. A nurse quickly entered the room, assessed Bandara's condition and called for a doctor. Efforts were made to revive his fading breath, and Bandara fought valiantly for his life. Despite numerous attempts to keep him alive, Bandara eventually succumbed.

"I am sorry. We couldn't save him," the doctor pronounced. "Did he have any family?"

"His wife passed away a few years ago. His son lives abroad and is expected to arrive later today," Priya said.

"May you find peace, Bandara," Rohan murmured, gently holding his hand. "Your courage and selflessness will forever be remembered. I can never repay the kindness you've shown."

In the stillness of the room, the weight of Bandara's sacrifice and his final moments lingered, a testament to the fragile nature of life.

"It's the Asuras who've taken Mira," Rohan said to Priya, leading the way to the hospital lobby.

"Let's step outside to talk. It might not be safe to discuss this here," Priya suggested in a hushed tone. They made their way out of the hospital, and she opened the car door. "Please, get in.

Mira is in real danger. She's with people who could pose a serious threat." She paused, concern etched on her face.

"Why would they abduct Mira? For ransom?"

"I don't think money is their motivation," Priya responded.

"What makes you think so?" Rohan probed.

"I've heard that some Asuras are quite affluent, but I can't say for certain," Priya explained.

"At the Godawaya site," Rohan recalled. "There was a woman who claimed to be a seer. She mentioned hearing voices. Strangely, she knew about the underwater flying machine before we had even examined the artefact. I was told that her name is Uru. She was at Karthigesu's presentation. There were two men with her. I saw these people at the resort a few days before Mira's abduction. Uru could be one of the suspects."

"Have you informed Inspector Chris about this?"

"No. I should have."

"Remember Bandara mentioning arrows? I've heard the Asuras, even today, practice ancient warrior skills. They're known for their courage, arrogance, thirst for revenge, and ruthlessness," Priya revealed.

"Poor Mira. I can't imagine what she might be going through."

"A few years ago," Priya said, "they made headlines for refusing to cooperate with the government. They follow their own rules, reject the country's laws, and call the government unnatural."

Chapter 15
The Search

> To reach this country none may dare
> Fallen from its old estate,
> Which she, whose fury naught can bear,
> Has left so desolate.
> And now my truthful tale is told
> How with accursed sway
> The spirit plagued this wood of old,
> And ceases not today.
>
> —Valmiki Ramayana, Book I, Canto XXVI

Priya introduced Uru Aththo to Chris and Rohan, explaining that she would lead them to the location where Mira was being held and emphasising that this was the only way to reach the Asuras.

"The seer." Rohan's curiosity tinged with suspicion. "You warned me to return home. Didn't you?"

"Yes," replied Uru, "I warned you to go home, but you didn't."

"How long have you been planning Mira's abduction?"

"Rohan," Priya intervened, "she will take us to Mira."

Rohan was overwhelmed by a whirlwind of emotions. He had seen Uru at the resort just a day before Mira was abducted. Could she be behind Mira's disappearance? He couldn't ignore the strange transformation he had witnessed in Uru, but he knew that sharing such a story would only invite scepticism. Despite his inner turmoil, he calmed himself and accepted Priya's suggestion—placing their trust in Uru seemed to be their only hope of rescuing Mira.

Uru led them into the tropical forest of the central highlands. Others followed her confident steps. The forest was a symphony of natural beauty, illuminated by vertical rays of yellowish-brown light that filtered through the blue sky above. Towering evergreen bushes stood as timeless sentinels, radiating an aura of grandeur.

A sweet and spicy fragrance permeated the air, adding a touch of enchantment to their journey. Surrounded by the untamed embrace of overgrown trees, shrubs, creepers, hills, and the chorus of birds, nature's exuberance obscured their path. Determined to rescue Mira, they forged ahead, navigating the intricate maze of tangled thorns and twisted grass, traversing the vast and foreboding woodland where dazzling blooms of countless varieties thrived.

Glimpses of sunlight filtered through the tree canopy, dappling the forest floor with patches of light and shadow. However beautiful the view was, a silent uneasiness filled Rohan's heart. He craved Mira's presence; nothing seemed to hold satisfaction without her. Every minute of delay could bring grave danger to her.

A profound stillness enveloped their surroundings within the vast wilderness they traversed, except for the persistent hum of buzzing mosquitoes and the distant chorus of insects. The intricacies of the path they treaded left little room for extensive conversations, resulting in hours of quiet contemplation.

As they ventured deeper into the forest, Uru's guidance proved indispensable, for the dense foliage concealed any traces of direction. Without her steady lead, they would have been lost in the labyrinthine expanse without any apparent clues to guide their way.

Years must have passed since grass overtook the once well-trodden track, obscuring its existence. In this forgotten path, lizards, monkeys, parrots, and butterflies forged their trails, navigating the complex maze at their leisurely pace as if time held no sway over their movements.

Black crows added their raucous calls, punctuating the air with their discordant cries. A gentle stream meandered through the forest, its soft marshy edges providing a tranquil respite amidst the wild surroundings.

With Uru leading the way, they followed closely, trusting her guidance yet trapped in their own illusions. Everything within the forest appeared unchanged, deceiving them into a false sense of familiarity, but that was not the case; they all knew that. The forest enveloped them, enclosing and unfolding like a series of interconnected Chinese boxes, each layer drawing them deeper into its profound depths.

The scenery shifted ceaselessly—the mountains, valleys, and narrow passages through dense rows of trees seemed to forever retreat as they advanced. In this ever-changing landscape, losing oneself was all too easy as the boundaries of reality blurred.

The gentle caress of the wind encircled them, creating an illusion that they were the sole human occupants of the forest, hidden from the world. Their journey led them to a serene river, where they paused, compelled to rest and seek solace in the tranquil surroundings.

Suddenly, a subtle rustling sound echoed from the underbrush, drawing their attention. Rohan's gaze shifted downward, only to meet the penetrating eyes of a magnificent snake coiled at his feet; he stood still.

He had seen snakes of all shapes and sizes, but this one seemed not only huge but also dangerous. He stared at its triangular-shaped head. It was a viper of the poisonous kind. The bands covering the entire length of its body wreathed rhythmically along a length of ground well over a meter long. Everyone stood motionless, watching the snake.

"My brother," Uru said, moving towards the serpent. "You shouldn't be here." She stretched her palm out. The snake looked at her waving hand; Uru held the snake gently but firmly enough, right behind the head, with her thumb on top of its head. Then, she walked towards a bush at a little distance and let it go.

The serpent's scales began to ripple and shift, rearranging themselves as if guided by some otherworldly force. The air crackled with an ancient energy as the snake transformed, shedding its serpentine form to emerge as a man. The metamorphosis was swift, as the snake's elongated body contorted and reshaped, morphing into limbs, torso, and a human visage.

The emerged man possessed a certain animalistic aura, his features reminiscent of the serpent's form. He stood upright, his eyes bearing the wisdom of ages, and the serpent's markings adorned his skin like intricate tattoos.

He spoke, "Who are these people? Why have you brought them here?" He was looking at Uru. His voice was imbued with a subtle hiss. "You know you are not supposed to bring these people here. Go away!" His eyes were both human and serpentine,

Inspector Chris saw the half-human, half-snake creature with a mix of professional caution. He quickly analysed the potential threat level posed by the creature. He pulled out his gun but was stopped by Priya.

"I am taking them to our village," Uru interrupted. "Kali asked me to bring them to her. Don't worry, my dear brother, I can manage this."

"Call if you need me." With a final nod, the man's form began to shift once more, his human semblance slowly transforming back into the serpentine shape from which he appeared. He slithered away and disappeared into the forest, leaving behind an atmosphere charged with a profound realisation that the boundaries between man and nature were far more fluid and enigmatic than they appeared.

"You saved our lives," Inspector Chris thanked Uru.

"My brother will not harm you until I tell him to." Uru walked towards the little stream of water.

"Why do you call him your brother?" Rohan asked.

"I grew up in the forest." She gathered her hair and tied it together in a knot atop her head. "Vasuki, whom you just met, is my elder brother. He possessed a unique heritage that set him apart from others. He was born with a mysterious birthmark, a swirling symbol etched upon his skin.

"As he grew older, the mark began to change, expanding and shifting in shape until it resembled the sinuous form of a serpent. It was then that the truth of his lineage was revealed—he was destined to become a half-man, half-snake."

As Vasuki and his sister Uru's story unfolded, Rohan, Priya, and Chris were transported to a world where serpents and humans coexisted.

The archaeologist in Rohan observed with keen scientific curiosity. He saw Vasuki as a potential archaeological marvel—an extraordinary discovery that could challenge existing beliefs about human and animal forms. His instinct was to document and study Vasuki, collecting evidence and data to substantiate the findings.

Priya's knowledge of mythologies, folklore and ancient beliefs made her associate the half-human half-snake with specific cultural narratives. She sought to understand the cultural context in which Vasuki existed and how it might relate to local beliefs or legends.

"Uru, you are a journalist," Priya asked. "Why don't you write your story?"

"Guess what happens then. Vasuki would be treated as an entertainment subject. I support my people," she continued, "who dwell in the forest. We are different. Now, you have even witnessed it. We are the original inhabitants of this island. The truth is that we love our freedom. We can't tolerate the genocide and all the crimes against our people. We need justice."

"Your people have sometimes gone a little too far," protested Inspector Chris. "A crime is a crime in the eyes of justice, whether committed by someone who lives in the city or the forest."

"I wish to disagree," Uru said.

"How old are you, Uru? If I may ask," Rohan enquired.

"I've been here since the beginning of time. My body has information that is thousands of years old. I don't need much; all I want is a free life. I get hundreds of emails asking for information about my people. I don't answer any of them. The streams and dense, lush forest of the ancient range still exist; this is our home."

"Kidnapping is a crime," repeated Inspector Chris. "How do we deal with that?"

"This is our land, and we have our own laws," Uru argued.

So far, in that vast tract of wilderness, Rohan had found no clue of Mira's kidnappers. They sat under a tree and ate the food they had brought. At such a moment, it seemed as if the whole country lay buried in eternal sleep, not a sound rising from the forest except the rippling of the river. Birds, beasts and humans appeared silent alike. The sound of the rivulet and feeble murmuring warned them of imminent danger.

The sun was just going down, spreading a red glory across the sky. They heard an elephant scream and saw it rushing with an uplifted trunk and tail against its colossal body. A mahout drove and controlled the tamed elephant. It slowed down near the river, drank water, and played with the mahout.

"I think we should camp here and continue our journey in the morning." Uru lit a campfire and talked about her encounter with wild animals, piecing together her experiences. Soon, it turned dark.

Rohan woke up in the morning with more confidence than he had expected. Chris had already lit the fire again and made breakfast for everyone. Later, they packed their things hurriedly and walked away from the river. "We will soon reach the village," Uru asserted after a few hours.

"I have heard that the Asuras move from one place to another. Is that true?" Priya asked.

"Hush." Uru signalled. She climbed up the gigantic ancient tree like a cheetah. "I can see the Asuras from here. We are not far away from the village."

Chapter 16
Kali

To Lanka's shore has bridged his way
And hither leads his wild array.
I know your might, in battle, tried,
Fighting and conquering by my side.
Why now, when such a foe is near,
Looks eye to eye in silent fear.
He ceased, his mother's sire well-known
For wisdom in the council shown,
Malyavan, sage and faithful guide.

—Valmiki Ramayana, Book VI, Canto XXV

The Asuras' village stood as a fortified stronghold, protected by towering walls and grand gates, nestled amidst a dense forest. Atop a small hill, a big house crafted from flat stones commanded attention, encircled by a cluster of smaller dwellings. Adjacent to the main house, a partly open wooden hangar suggested the possible presence of a flying machine within.

The village landscape revealed signs of labour and resilience, with huts, sheds, and cultivated fields reflecting the villagers' diligent efforts. A steady water supply streamed down from the lofty slopes of the mountain, sustaining the houses and their inhabitants. Strategically positioned, the village was designed to hinder any approach or departure without keen observation.

"The natives are alert even in their sleep," Uru cautioned. "A tiny sound of alarm, men and women will stand afoot surrounding us, ready for battle if necessary. Now that I have led you to the Asuras, my job is done. I will see you later."

"Wait," shouted Priya, but Uru was too quick to disappear.

Seeing strangers entering the village premises, men, women, and children ran back and forth, seemingly confused and frightened. Gradually, the disorder diminished, and in a few minutes, the chieftain and the other notable people assembled in the lodge in grave consultation.

The villagers crowded in a body around the council lodge, impatiently awaiting instructions from their chief, the guardian of a forgotten era. They embraced their ancient lineage while navigating the complexities of the modern world. There was anger mingled with quiet restlessness and unconcealed amazement.

Living in harmony with nature, the Asuras seemed to have found solace in remote and untouched landscapes, preserving their connection to the earth and its spirits. Their deep, piercing eyes reflected knowledge passed down through generations as if they held the universe's secrets within their gazes.

Blending colourful textiles and intricate patterns with modern fabrics and accessories, they were adorned with feathers, beads and handcrafted jewellery. Each piece told a story, a testament to their heritage and the struggles they had endured.

The chief of the Asuras was a woman of powerful build and a great shoulder width. Her eyes were in a state of native roughness or certain weariness, sloping lines of distress, dim and pale but of power and strength. The chief bore the boomerang and a knife, like a warrior, similar to Uru. She hid her eyes in sorrow for a moment. Then, recovering her self-possession, she faced her companions.

"The Great Spirit is angry with his children," she spoke. A grave silence prevailed. There was something strange about her appearance. Her face was split down the middle, with one side looking perfectly normal while the other appeared ethereal.

Chris, Priya and Rohan stood mesmerised by the surreal sight before them. It was as if the woman had been caught between two worlds, one real and one imagined.

They could see the contrast more clearly as she turned to face them fully. The left side of her face looked like any other person's, with clear skin, defined features, and a natural complexion. But the right side of her face seemed almost unreal as if it had been sculpted from a dream, translucent and otherworldly.

"She is Uru," Rohan announced.

"How can she be Uru? She looks different, doesn't she?" Chris protested.

"I have seen Uru take the form of the chief, believe me," Rohan said.

"Look over there, Rohan," Chris whispered, pointing his finger at her. "There she is. You were wrong about Uru and the chief being the same person." Uru came walking towards the chief. She had changed her clothes and blended into the looks of her people. "That's Uru, is she not? But look at their chief. Is she some mythical being? Or I am imagining."

"So, if Uru and the chief are two different people, then Uru must've taken the form of the chief only to confuse me," Rohan muttered.

Next to the chief stood a young man Rohan recognised. He bore a strong resemblance to the chief—they looked like mother and son, with the natural differences that come with age. Beside him stood Uru. *She must be the chief's daughter*, thought Rohan.

"Since the brutal death of Ravana," the chief continued, "we've been living in secret, tucked away from the rest of the world. No one can find us; no one knows us. If, by chance, someone discovers our village, we do not allow them to enter. We do not marry anyone else but the Asuras.

"We are all by ourselves. It is not as simple as it sounds, but an age-old shame and guilt have remained within us. We cannot bear the rage and pain any longer. Ravana is here, always here, present among us. I hear his voice. He talks to me. We must liberate our ancestor, Ravana.

"I can hear and see everything in the human realm and the underworld pretty much all the time. In the human realm, I'm omniscient. I can choose to take different forms. Surprised? Yes, me too. In the beginning, I felt excited when I learned I could look like a tree or a monkey or take the form of anyone in our village. Imagine you suddenly realised you could breathe underwater.

"Only the single-minded overcome the reflex panic and yield to the body's fit. I am one of the single-minded. So, I took the form of animals. Birds were the obvious first choice—for the bird-eye's view. Yes, I thoroughly enjoy flying." She paused, seeming to hold the power to connect between the seen and unseen, as if she were a guardian of ancient wisdom and keeper of forgotten realms.

"But it's not fun anymore," she continued, "especially when I know my destiny does not change. I will always belong to the Asuras, and we are cursed."

Chris, Priya, and Rohan stood before the chief. Their gazes locked with hers; they could feel an indescribable connection. It was as if she embodied the essence of the Asuras' ancient lineage, a bridge between their mortal existence and the vast unseen world of the Asuras.

"I disguise myself," the chief continued, "when I step out of this village; probably, many of you do the same. We all hide our true selves one way or the other, don't we? But we are different. We are the Asuras; never forget that. We do not tolerate made-up narratives or biased stories about us. In all honesty, we do not desire publicity.

"Even back during the time of Ravana, stories were not

honestly written. They were one-sided, nothing but political propaganda. Don't you agree with me? They did not write the whole story of Ravana as it was. Whatever they wrote was not him, not our ancestor Ravana. They used his name. He couldn't do anything. He had no choice.

"Now, I've got some moves. But even if I didn't, there is no reason to let go of the human effort in the land of propaganda. Incarnation requires a strong will and cool head—well, a cool mind until an actual head is available.

"What mattered to the Asuras," she continued, "was that our ancestor Ravana could not reach heaven. He is trapped in the underworld, neither dead nor reborn. We, the Asuras, did everything possible to free him. For Ravana's sake, we created our world, waiting for our hero to return home to give him his dues. Ravana was wrong in thinking that the war against the Aryans would be okay—but there's no telling this story without contradiction."

The chief spoke for a while. Chris, Rohan and Priya stood listening. "Come here," she told them, in a death-like calmness. "Come closer, I wish to speak to you. Inspector Chris should leave the village at once."

Hearing those words, Chris became agitated. "I will arrest all of them right now. I will charge them for murder."

"You do not have enough proof to call them murderers, Chris," Priya objected.

"Inspector, please wait outside. Please. Do it for Mira's sake," Rohan begged.

"Do you understand the nature of the chief's wishes?" Inspector Chris asked. "Call me if you are in trouble. I'll wait outside."

Rohan followed the instructions given to him by the chief.

Priya walked together with Rohan. The chief of the Asuras rose slowly from her seat and stood for a while, silent and motionless. "I am Kali," she said, laying her hand firmly upon Rohan's arm as if willing to draw his utmost attention.

A movement Rohan firmly resisted by freeing the arm from her grasp. She was as real as anyone he had ever met. Despite her half face, there was something deeply human about her, something that spoke to him on a fundamental level.

"I had to make sure you could be trusted," Kali whispered. Then, she told them all, "I was born as a chief among the Asuras. My father saw the suns of fifty summers and the rain of fifty monsoons that ran in the streams before the white man entered the woods. He said he was a friend who had come to learn our way of life but was a rascal."

"Where is my wife?" Rohan agitated.

"Was it the fault of my father?" Kali continued, ignoring Rohan's words, "Who cheated who? Who made us villains? The white man."

"Am I answerable to that? I'm not responsible for the acts of others. And what are these white men all about? You sound like a racist. Besides, I am not even a white man," Rohan protested.

"Kali is our leader and not a fool," the man beside her added. "She never says anything without sense. The Great Spirit has given her wisdom. We know that you live in a white man's country."

"What, then, you want me to do if a white man cheated you? Why have you kidnapped my wife? Where is she? I would like to see her at once."

"Quiet," ordered Kali. "The white man has stolen our manuscript. Return it to us, and we will let your wife go."

"Which white man? What manuscript?"

"Return the manuscript," ordered Kali. "Return what belongs

to us." She held a photograph in her hand and handed it to Rohan. It was an old black-and-white photograph of a white man posing with the Asura people.

Priya looked at the photograph and whispered, "He is Egon von Eickstedt, the German anthropologist."

"This white man has taken our manuscript of the flying ship," Kali said.

"How is this related to kidnapping my wife?"

"You live in a white man's country. You are interested in artefacts; he was also interested in artefacts. My father had seen him take away many old objects. His spirit was then in the clouds. He cheated us and took away the manuscript without our knowledge. It belongs to us. The spirit of an Asura is never drunk, and we haven't forgotten."

"I am in no way related to the white man you are talking about. This man in the photograph must even be dead by now. How do you expect me to find your manuscript?"

Kali shook her head, forbidding the question.

"If you have something against a white man, let me tell you this. I was born in India, and my wife is Indian. Let my wife go. We haven't done anything to harm you."

"Even worse. We dislike Indians. Before the white man stole our manuscript, an Indian was here to study our flying ship. My grandfather gave him all the information he needed. The fool built his ship but didn't succeed. When he wanted to meet my grandfather, he flew over the Indian Ocean, crossing India's border with Lanka.

"His plane crashed in the ocean. If he hadn't died in the crash, he would have had his eyes set on the manuscript as he tried several times to take it away from my father. So, I do not have a special liking for Indians either."

Rohan thought about Shivkar Talpade, the pilot whose flying machine had crashed into the Indian Ocean. The archaeological team had lifted it from the Godaway site, which was the very reason that had brought him to Lanka in the first place. He and his wife should have never come to this island. "You kidnapped my wife for a manuscript that is probably of no use to you today?" Rohan asked angrily.

"It is very useful to us. Even today," retaliated the chief.

"Are you planning to build more flying machines and sell them to the world? Who would buy your machines? Why do you need the manuscript?"

"An Asura would never share his knowledge with the outside world. The manuscript belongs to us. Our ancestor, the mighty Ravana, has written it for us. We own that secret knowledge and are the only people who know how to decipher it."

"You claim to be the descendants of Ravana, who kidnapped Sita? Now, you kidnap my wife, Mira. Does kidnapping run in your family?"

"What do you know about Ravana's bloodline? He was the most able yet unfortunate king of all time. We are proud of our ancestors. Many years after the death of Ravana, Valmiki wrote the Ramayana, making Ravana a villain, and the world believed his story. Valmiki's motivation was propaganda, to glorify the Aryans, but at the cost of the Asuras.

"Since then, all my ancestors have lived a life of isolation. If every one of us, alive or dead, weep for him, then he will be allowed to return to heaven. If anyone speaks against him or refuses to cry, then he will remain in the netherworld.

"Ravana has returned. He has made himself aware of us and poured an ocean of love into which we sported and splashed. Since he is infinitely loveable, to know him was to love him. So, it went on for what would have been thousands of years. Asuras, we may be, but no one gets the credit for the discovery of freedom. Millennia followed after the Great War.

"We, the Asuras, have stayed together. Our voices stirred, and we tried new things. Our voices move through the clear waters of the ocean like a turbulent underwater current. I swear by the Great Spirit of Ravana, who speaks to us even today. I will kill every man who brings disgrace to the great Ravana."

"Did you kill Professor Shastry? Did you kill Karthigesu? Only because they wrote about Ravana?"

"Do not ask questions. Find the manuscript. Otherwise, we have your wife. It takes only a few seconds to take the life out of her."

"What if I don't find the manuscript?" Rohan agitated.

"Then your wife will stay with us; she will become an Asura."

"How would I know that my wife is still alive?"

"You must trust me."

Kali showed an unaltered purpose. She signalled with her hand as if to close the conference. Rohan had no choice but to comply. The chief, her son, and Uru instantly left the spot. Rohan walked to Inspector Chris, who sat outside, drinking alcohol from his flask. Just like Rohan, even Chris looked agitated. Rohan's voice fell, and he was frazzled. Priya explained the situation to Inspector Chris.

"I can arrest the chief right now and end this turmoil," Chris proposed angrily.

"Which I think is absolute nonsense; we don't even know where they have imprisoned Mira. If you arrest the chief now, we will never be able to find my wife. I have no choice but to find the manuscript," Rohan said.

"I will go with you," Priya volunteered.

Chapter 17
Frankfurt

> There stood before their wondering eyes
> A fiend broad-chested, huge of size.
> A vast misshapen trunk they saw
> In height surpassing nature's law.
>
> —Valmiki Ramayana, Book III, Canto LXX

On the Hermitage Island, the Buddhist monk Assaji was reading. It was close to midnight when he heard footsteps. He saw someone walking near his room—a man dressed in black. Extinguishing his cigar, he slowly padded onto the portico. Assaji recognised Arthur Hoffmann, Professor Shastry's friend who had frequently visited the monastery. Hoffmann held some keys in his hand, which he was using to open the door and stealthily creeping inside the room. There was no sound except for the singsong rasping of crickets in the nearby forest.

Assaji followed Hoffmann. He could hear shuffling footsteps from the room. When he peeped through the window, he saw Hoffmann with a torch, searching Professor Shastry's room. Assaji returned to his room on the same floor, opposite Professor Shastry's room.

He stood behind the window, hiding and watching. A few minutes later, Hoffmann came out of the room, left the building and disappeared into the woods, camouflaged by the colour of his clothes against the dark background.

Assaji tried to call Inspector Chris but found his phone turned off. Perplexed, he went to bed, pondering why Hoffmann had chosen to visit discreetly in the dead of night rather than during daylight hours. What could he be searching for in the professor's room? Assaji speculated that it must be the copper plates he had seen and heard the professor discuss.

In the morning, Inspector Chris returned Assaji's call, expressing frustration over his phone's low battery that had gone unnoticed when it shut off. After their conversation, Chris swiftly ended the call and immediately transmitted Hoffmann's description to police headquarters across Lanka and to all airports and port offices. The search for Arthur Hoffmann escalated nationwide.

Accompanied by a fingerprint expert, Chris travelled to the Hermitage Island. However, their efforts yielded no trace of Hoffmann's fingerprints within the monastery. By late afternoon, Chris received a phone call from the airport. Hoffmann had departed Lanka, evading capture.

Although Chris refrained from criticising the efficiency of the police department, a flicker of desperation gleamed in his eyes upon receiving the information from airport authorities that Hoffmann had travelled to Berlin. In response to Chris's request, the airport authorities provided him with a copy of Hoffmann's passport, photograph, address, and phone number.

It was a stormy night when Priya and Rohan sat on the plane that took off from Colombo airport. Rohan gazed out of the window; his heart shattered at the thought of Mira being held captive by her kidnappers. She was now a mere puppet, trapped in the relentless iron hands of the Asura, leaving no room for escape. The lights twinkled across the expanse of the island of Lanka, a sight that felt familiar and strangely distant.

Leaving Mira alone in Lanka under such dangerous circumstances weighed heavily on Rohan's conscience. Still, he knew that this journey was essential to rescue her from the clutches of those who sought to harm her.

Rohan summarised his whole life to Priya, or that's what she thought he did. He spoke with an unusual level of openness. Bit by bit, she gained insight into his childhood, discovering his fondness for puzzle games. His journey through university recounting his academic pursuits and research papers. He painted a vivid picture of his time at various archaeological sites, describing his meticulous skills as a digger and the thrill of unearthing ancient artefacts. He was a man who woke up each morning and fearlessly dove into the intricate maze of history, driven by his passion and curiosity to uncover the secrets of the past.

He didn't hesitate to reveal how he had met his wife, Mira. Even in the face of adversity, he carried a glimmer of hope, believing in the possibility of finding her again.

"I fail to understand," he said. "If Egon von Eickstedt had taken the manuscript from the Asura, why was the coffer that held the manuscript found at the site?"

"Remember what Director Bandara had told us," she answered. "The Asuras gave the manuscript to Eickstedt as a deal with Hitler. The Asuras wanted Hitler to overthrow the British and help them regain their freedom in Lanka. I believe Eickstedt left the coffer."

"Do you know anything about the Vaimanika Shastra? Who wrote it and when?"

"Based on documented history," Priya answered, "Maya Asura was an architect famous for his skills in arts and science. He knew how to build a flying machine. According to one version of the Vedas, Patanjali wrote the Vaimanika Shastra, which is aeronautical science.

"Maya Asura, who was against writing down the secret knowledge, threw the manuscript into the fire. He declared a death sentence against Patanjali and locked him up in a cell. Patanjali begged and pleaded, but Maya Asura's decision remained unchanged. As a reaction to the harsh penalty, Patanjali decided to rewrite the Vaimanika Shastra for the eternal glory of humankind.

"He had only three nights left before his execution. Near the first midnight, he realised that he couldn't complete the task alone, so, through one of his disciples, he sent word to Ravana, who came to meet Patanjali. The monk dictated the words to Ravana who wrote them down."

"Are you referring to Ravana, the ruler of Lanka?"

"Yes, the one and only Ravana. Patanjali gave credit of writing the Vaimanika Shastra to Ravana."

"Who was Patanjali?"

"Little is known about Patanjali's early life and education. He was a scientist born into a wealthy family. Some say he was a blood relative of Maya Asura. Patanjali may have travelled to Greece. Upon his return, he took part in improving the monastery at Taxila. A mutilated manuscript found in Taxila claims that he conducted courses in science and mathematics, researched flying machines together with Maya Asura for about twelve years and that they had even succeeded in building such a machine."

"The fragmented script says," Priya opened her laptop and read:

> *The great flying bird of light material, strong and durable was the body of the flying ship. Underneath the flying ship was a mercury engine fixed with its iron heating apparatus. By the power latent in the mercury, which sets the driving whirlwind in motion, a man sitting inside may travel a great distance in the sky.*

> *The movements of the Vimana are such that it can vertically ascend, vertically descend, and slant forward and backwards. With the help of these ships, human beings can fly in the air and heavenly beings can come down to earth.*

She closed her laptop and kept it aside. "Patanjali's most important work," Priya continued, "was the treatise on physics and metaphysics. His work itself is lost in time. Towards the end of his life, he became paranoid and threatened Maya Asura. That could also be the reason for his death sentence.

"Patanjali was an Asura," Priya continued, "a teacher in a monastery run by King Maya. Archaeologists have found a room-like structure at the site of Taxila, which they believe holds the remains of Patanjali. The sealed room had stone slab doors with stone plugs in the holes. Opening the room and clearing the ruins took almost three years. Surprisingly, in 1910, the skeletal remains of a woman were found in the room. Who was she? Was Patanjali a woman? No one knows."

"Very interesting," Rohan said. "If Ravana wrote the manuscript, it must have been around four thousand BCE. The text must have been rewritten on new material several times."

"Yes. We know that palm leaf paper has a life of about seven hundred years before it starts deteriorating," Priya added. "In the past, monasteries like Nalanda and Taxila rewrote manuscripts once in seven hundred years or before, when they showed signs of decay. After rewriting, the scholars disposed of the old manuscripts in an orthodox ritualistic style. The age-old tradition exists even today. There is evidence that suggests that the Vaimanika Shastra was found in Taxila hidden away from the public eyes."

"What evidence do we have, Priya?"

"Taxila, one of the earliest universities, held many manuscripts in its library. Among them, a document discovered there mentions the Vaimanika Shastra alongside other texts."

"It must be a lengthy one. Where is this list today?"

"At the Bhandarkar Orient Research Institute in Pune," she said, "but I'm not sure if it is still there."

King Ashoka had moved the Taxila library to Nalanda University in present-day Bihar, where he kept all the manuscripts of secret knowledge locked away in an underground hidden library. He appointed Buddhist monks to protect the collection, and it is believed that the Vaimanika Shastra, along with other manuscripts, remained hidden at Nalanda.

In 1193, Nalanda was ransacked and destroyed by a Turkish army. The great library was so vast that it burned for three months after the invaders set fire. The monasteries were looted, and the monks were driven from the site. However, the monks, appointed by King Ashoka, continued their legacy of selecting successors who cared for the secret manuscripts. As the library burned, they fled Nalanda with the manuscripts they had vowed to protect until their deaths. One monk carried the Vaimanika Shastra to Lanka, ensuring the manuscript's survival on the island.

"It all makes sense to me now," Rohan said. "History is full of mysteries."

"So it seems," Priya replied.

The flight landed in Frankfurt, and they took the train to Berlin. As they arrived in the city, dark clouds veiled the sky, hinting at an imminent rainfall. They walked along the riverside until they reached the Mon Bijou bridge. The crystalline waters of the river Spree encircled Museum Island, a renowned collection of splendid *Gruenderzeit* architectural masterpieces.

Along the pedestrian path, a carpet of dry leaves coated the ground, mirroring the autumnal hues of the surrounding trees. Continuing their walk, they passed by the majestic Berliner Dom, eventually arriving at their destination—a towering ten-storey hotel. Only in the late afternoon were they finally able to grab a hurried lunch at the restaurant. Once the waiter took their orders, Priya turned to Rohan and asked, "Have you ever visited Berlin before?"

"Yes," he answered. "As a tourist, I was here with Mira once."

"And you?"

"I've been to Berlin before," she said, her voice tinged with sorrow. "This city holds countless memories of my husband. His absence is something I'll never grow accustomed to."

The waiter placed the food on the table.

"I understand what you're going through," he replied. "If archaeologists and police have something in common, it's logic. Investigating a crime can be similar to discovering an artefact."

His phone rang. "Hello?" he said, answering.

"This is Inspector Chris speaking. Have you reached Berlin?"

"Yes, we have. I think we will start our search tomorrow."

"Do you know anyone by the name Arthur Hoffmann?"

"No, never heard of him. Who is he?"

"He is an acquaintance of Professor Shastry's, who visited him just before his murder. The monk, Assaji, saw him creeping into Professor Shastry's room at the Hermitage Island in the middle of the night. He was probably searching for the copper plates."

"Have you arrested him, Chris?"

"Couldn't, he had already flown to Berlin. Since you are in Berlin, could you find out more about this man?"

"What do you know about him other than his name?"

"I will send you his photograph, telephone number and address."

"Why don't you come to Germany, Chris?"

"My job doesn't support this. I won't be able to arrest him without the backing of the German government, which could be a problem."

"I'll do anything to solve this and find Mira. It seems like the case has grown complicated."

Chris hung up the phone.

"Do you know this man, Priya?" Rohan asked, showing her Chris's photograph of Arthur Hoffmann.

"Yes, I know him."

"According to Chris, this man is an acquaintance of Professor Shastry. What do you know about him?"

"I've been living in Germany for some time and had the chance to meet Arthur Hoffman a few times. He's a fascinating character—businessman, investor, antique collector and adventurer all in one. One of his prized possessions is a model of the first hot air balloon developed by the French Montgolfier Brothers. In 1783, it became the first balloon to carry human passengers on a free flight. As far as I know, Hoffmann's private collection includes over nine hundred manuscripts in various languages."

She paused, as though trying to recall. "In 1995, Hoffmann made headlines when he crossed the Pacific Ocean from Japan to Arctic Canada in a balloon, breaking a speed record. He even attempted to circumnavigate the globe by balloon, with a record-breaking flight from Morocco to Hawaii. There's more to him, but those are the highlights."

She smiled slightly, her eyes distant with the memory. "When Hoffmann visited our house a few years ago, he made quite an impression. He's a tall man with sharp eyes and a striking purple nose. I've heard he suffers from a chronic skin condition that causes the redness in his face."

"Why wouldn't he just get surgery?" Rohan asked.

"Well, that's the thing. When he was a child, he suffered from seizures, and he was afraid that any surgery could bring them back. He's very self-conscious about his appearance and refuses to be photographed because of it. I've seen him several times at auctions with my husband, Davis. Davis was writing a book about him and took his photograph at one of the auctions. That's why Hoffmann came to our house personally—he wanted Davis to promise not to publish the photo."

She leaned forward, her voice lowering in excitement. "His collections are incredible—ancient flying machines, rare manuscripts, and photographs. In a recent radio interview, Hoffmann mentioned buying a flying machine based on Leonardo da Vinci's Codex on the Flight of Birds. But he also said something intriguing—he claimed that the only thing missing in his collection was the South Asian flying machine. What he meant, of course, was Ravana's flying machine."

"Interesting," Rohan said. "Do you think we can meet him? We can question him about his connections with Professor Shastry."

"Give me his phone number, Rohan; let me try calling him. I hope he remembers me as Davis' wife." She dialled the number and walked away. After a while, she returned and said, "His secretary told me that he is abroad and will be back before the end of this week. We will have to try again later."

Chapter 18
Berlin

> There will I enter in, and through
> The tangled shade my search renews.
> Be glory to the host on high,
> The Sun and Moon who light the sky,
> The Vasus and the Maruts' train,
> Ádityas and the As'vins twain.
> So may I win success, and bring
> The lady back with triumphing,
>
> —Valmiki Ramayana, Book V, Canto XIII

By the time Rohan's watch showed eleven, the ashtray was full of cigarette ends, and the wine bottle stood empty among various books and papers. After a strong wind came rain, as if the weather had retorted to his thoughts. He was unsteady; everything from his thoughts to his feelings was like disjointed jigsaw puzzle pieces.

Engulfed by the rhythmic sound of rain and the heavy void left by Mira's absence, he sank into the sofa, staring out the window as he struggled to piece together his scattered thoughts. A flood of reflections overwhelmed him—the puzzle of Professor Shastry's death intertwined with the mysteries of Karthigesu's demise and the tragic end of the director.

The recollection of copper plates, which contained the stories of the Asuras' and the remarkable artefacts recovered from the depths of the Indian Ocean occupied his mental landscape. The Godawaya archaeological site and the seer Uru, who had warned him to return home, loomed large in his thoughts. Uru had then led them to the land of the Asuras.

Contemplating their arduous path in search of Mira, his thoughts extended to Kali, the intimidating Asuras' chief, with her overwhelming appearance and unyielding demands for Mira's release. The words 'Vaimanika Shastra' escaped his lips, a testament to the lost knowledge of ancient aeronautical science.

It struck him that Kali's reaction could not have been a mere coincidence, hinting at zealous efforts to obtain the manuscript long before. With her crafty nature, she had orchestrated the kidnapping of Mira. Who was responsible for all the deaths? Was it Kali herself, or had she commissioned another person to carry out her orders? Despite the absence of concrete evidence linking Kali to the murders, the emergence of Arthur Hoffmann added yet another layer of complexity to the case.

An ancient manuscript, more than two millennia old, gave him a sleepless night. Whatever the results of this search would be, Ravana, the man who had written the manuscript, could not have foreseen the future, or could he? Disquieting questions surfaced in his mind. What was the meaning of all this? Challenged by the whereabouts of the manuscript, it was up to him to decide where to start the hunt for it.

In the past, he had thoroughly enjoyed the thrill of discovering ancient artefacts—it had always been a source of joy for him. But now, with Mira's life at stake, the urgency to find the manuscript and to succeed in his mission weighed heavily on him. He hoped coming to Berlin would bring him closer to the ancient script. It was a matter of life and death. Feeling uneasy, he turned on all the lights, hoping to drive away the bad spirits surrounding him.

The morning was cool and fresh, with the sun casting a gentle, golden light. Rohan was already seated in the breakfast room when Priya came down the stairs.

"Good morning," he greeted her.

"Morning, Rohan. Do we have plans for today?"

"Yes, we're heading to the library. It's nearby."

"And what do we do there?"

"We're looking for information about Egon von Eickstedt."

The Berlin State Library was on the same street as the hotel. Built around 1660, it was a magnificent building with its large windows, high arch roof, and elegant lamps. The spacious hall was vast and serene, with rows of shelves filled with books bathed in soft natural light streaming through tall windows and the soft hum of students studying. The air carried a faint scent of aged paper and knowledge. Patrons quietly moved about, their footsteps muffled by the carpeted floor.

"Rohan," Priya whispered, standing by the anthropology section. "Look. Egon von Eickstedt has written these books. Here's his master's thesis on human races. They're all in German. Would you like me to translate them for you?"

"Yes, please," he replied.

They sat at a wooden table by a window, surrounded by stacks of reference materials.

Priya flipped through pages before whispering, "Eickstedt was born in 1892 in Prussia. Rohan, what specifically would you like to know about his work?"

"Anything related to his South Asian expedition."

"This book," she continued, "has details on Eickstedt's Andaman expedition with photographs. The body measurements he did on people and his writings on ethnographic-geographical facts. Of all the material he had produced, only this report has survived the Second World War. Eickstedt founded a journal called *Human Biology, a comparative study.*"

"That's interesting, Priya. When I researched Eickstedt yesterday over the internet, I found that the most important international institutions interested in the Andaman and India have not even mentioned Eickstedt and his work. I guess his work has fallen low. I hope we get close to what we want."

"Listen, Rohan, let me read further. Eickstedt went to India with a team of scientists to conduct anthropological investigations on Indian prisoners sentenced by the British for sedition or similar crimes. The British Raj in India showed a special interest in his studies; probably, they saw it as a chance to degrade the Indian race to justify their rule over India."

"But, Priya, during late 1920, when the anti-German feelings had not completely died following the First World War, how did Eickstedt, a German, manage to get permission from the British authorities for fieldwork in its colony?"

"No idea, but he did go to India. Look, it's even mentioned here that he was sponsored by Theodor Mollison and the Anthropological Society of Leipzig."

"Leipzig," Rohan repeated. "I think someone's watching us," he whispered. "That man over there, by the bookshelves. Can you see him? We must keep our voices down."

Priya followed Rohan's gaze discreetly, her eyes widening in concern. The young man, slim and tall, had a ponytail and beard. He looked like a European. She nodded subtly, acknowledging the potential threat. "He might be eavesdropping on us," she murmured. "We need to be careful, Rohan."

The stranger, noticing the change in their behaviour, adjusted his position to maintain visual contact with Rohan and Priya. His eyes narrowed, suggesting a determined pursuit. The library remained silent, save for the rustling of pages and the occasional sound of a keyboard or a pen scribbling a note.

Rohan and Priya remained vigilant, aware of the young man's persistent presence, determined to protect their research and uncover the truth hidden within the pages of history. Their every move was calculated and guarded.

She continued reading, "Eickstedt travelled across South Asia over two years, covering thousands of kilometres. During his journey, he collected more than two thousand antique objects from the Asian subcontinent."

"Is there any information about the artefacts themselves?"

"There are no specific details about the artefacts. It mentions that he invested years in meticulously analysing and documenting each piece. The majority of the book focuses on his findings related to *Rassenkunde*."

"What does *Rassenkunde* mean?"

"It's a German word for the study of the human race."

"Priya, we should note it and cross-reference it with the other sources. Can you give me the names associated with Eickstedt? I'll make a note of them." He took the pen in his hand.

"Felix von Luschan—he was Eickstedt's professor in Berlin. Later, Eickstedt worked with Eugen Fischer at the Institute of Anatomy in Freiburg."

"Slow down, Priya. Who is Eugen Fischer?"

"Eugen Fischer was one of those responsible for the Nazi theories of racial hygiene that finally led to the extermination of Jews, the killing of half a million gypsies and the compulsory sterilisation of hundreds of thousands racially defective and mentally ill." She paused.

"In 1924," she continued, "Eickstedt became the leader of the anthropology section in the natural history museum in Vienna. He was a member of the Nazi party."

"Then," Priya continued, "Eickstedt worked with Theodor Mollison in Munich. We found his name in another document. Do you remember it? Theodor Mollison sponsored Eickstedt on the expedition to India."

Rohan noted the name Theodor Mollison and highlighted it by underlining it several times.

"Eickstedt got promoted as professor by the Nazi party. He continued to work for them in their research on race theories. Rohan, there are some papers by Eickstedt on the study of race. I don't think we should get into the details of racism. So, that is all about Eickstedt. There is no more information on him." Priya closed the book.

"That's incredible," Rohan said. His gaze shifted slightly, catching sight of the mysterious stranger lurking near the bookshelves. The stranger's intense eyes were fixed on them, and his ears seemed tuned to their conversation.

"Eyes watching," Rohan whispered.

"Look at these photographs," Priya spoke softly. "See, this is Eickstedt with Heinrich Himmler. This photograph was taken in 1944."

"Are we talking about the infamous Heinrich Himmler, the head of the *Schutzstaffel* Protection Squad SS for short?"

"Yes, Rohan, that's him."

Rohan sprang to his feet. "Let me go check the catalogues in the Asian manuscript section." He walked away. After a while, he returned and sat next to Priya again, looking at the words he had scribbled on his notepad.

"Any luck?" she asked.

"No luck so far. This library holds around forty thousand fragments of Asian manuscripts. I've encountered texts in Old Turkish, Iranian, Sanskrit, Prakrit, Chinese, Mongolian, and

Tibetan. In the Sanskrit, Brahmi and Prakrit sections, most texts are on paper, but some are written on other materials like silk, leather, birch bark or palm leaves. There are Sanskrit texts in Brahmi script, fragments of the Buddhist canon, Sanskrit grammar, Buddhist dramas, medical texts, a Sanskrit dictionary, and various Buddhist writings. But so far, not a single clue about what we are looking for."

As their voices lowered, blending into the library's hushed ambience, the stranger intended to listen to their every word.

"What do we do now, Rohan?"

"Check for writings, rare and antique," Rohan said, "something you and I have never seen or heard before, something that can give us a clue about the Vaimanika Shastra. Have you found any other information on Eickstedt?"

"Yes, I have. I want to read this for you. When the Nazis came to power, Eickstedt tried to grab the opportunity. The Nazis rejected him for reasons unknown. Then, Eickstedt faced serious political problems, though it is not clear why and what. A research assistant, Joachim Fuchs, is the only person alive. We need to go back to the archives in the library and try to get this person's address."

"That's fantastic information you are giving me, Priya. I hope it helps us find the manuscript." As Rohan spoke, he wrote the name Joachim Fuchs on his notepad.

"Let's go to the Indology section. Priya, search for any information on Joachim Fuchs?"

Joachim Fuch's name was mentioned under the institution's history, the University of Munich. After a while, Priya read, "Joachim Fuchs worked as the Head of Indology from 1961 to 1986. He has authored papers even after his retirement. The address given here is Berlin. That's what I call coincidence."

"Excellent job, Priya."

"What's our next move?" Priya turned her gaze towards Rohan.

"I'm considering heading to Leipzig."

"Leipzig?"

"Yes," Rohan said, "I hope to see the artefacts collected by Eickstedt. We might even find the Vaimanika Shastra."

"Alright. What if we don't find the Vaimanika Shastra? What then, Rohan?"

"Then we go to either Mainz or Breslau, following the footsteps of Eickstedt," Rohan answered.

They stepped into the warm sunlight outside the library onto the bustling city streets. The man from the library followed them at a distance. Rohan and Priya walked briskly, occasionally glancing over their shoulders, their minds preoccupied with the stranger's unsettling presence. They subtly increased their pace, weaving through the crowd while keeping a watchful eye on the stranger. They made a series of quick turns, ducking into narrow alleyways and dodging through side streets. Assuming the man did not see them, they entered the hotel building and retired to their rooms.

Chapter 19
The Nazis

When there is a disturbance or external intervention
to the principles and laws of the universe,
I show Myself as the Power of eternal balancing.
To protect those in harmony and extinct the miscreants,
I incarnate Myself at every contingency of time.

—Bhagavad Gita Chapter IV Hymn VII and VIII

The following morning, during breakfast, Rohan suggested to meet Joachim Fuchs before heading for Leipzig. He picked up his phone and dialled the numbers he had written down. After a few rings, a male voice answered, introducing himself as Joachim Fuchs.

"Hello, Mr Fuchs. This is archaeologist Rohan Sharma. My colleague, Priya, and I have a keen interest in meeting with you to discuss your perspectives on the Aryan influence on the Nazis."

"I am an old man, Mr Sharma. I am not sure how I could be of any help to you. I avoid meeting people these days."

"I understand, Mr Fuchs. We have travelled a long distance and are searching for a missing manuscript. In our archaeological exploration in Lanka, we encountered some clues that led us here. I can provide you with more information when we meet."

"I am curious to learn about your discoveries. Would it be possible for you to visit my residence?"

"Certainly, any time," said Rohan.

"If you'd like, you can come over now. Please take note of my address."

Rohan jotted down the address and ended the call. "Let's go," he said to her.

As Rohan and Priya stepped onto the pavement, they were alarmed by the man's familiar figure with the ponytail and beard. Just a few meters away, he stood beneath a tall tree on the opposite side of the road.

With an air of confidence, he seemed engrossed in observing his surroundings, his gaze occasionally wandering from one point to another. Rohan and Priya, filled with a growing sense of unease, walked on the street, their eyes on high alert. The once bright sunlight now cast long shadows, creating an eerie backdrop for the unfolding events.

Around the corner, Rohan and Priya took a taxi, eager to meet Fuchs. They hoped the man with the ponytail would miss seeing them. The taxi driver manoeuvred through the bustling city streets.

Rohan turned his head to look out through the rear window. To his alarm, he noticed the same man trailing them in another car, his presence unpromisingly threatening. Fear tightened its grip on his heart, and his mind raced to comprehend the gravity of the situation.

The man's vehicle seemed to mimic their movements, maintaining an uncomfortable proximity. His car, like a shadowy spectre, followed their every turn. The distant cityscape that had once displayed the charm and energy now took on a foreboding quality, amplifying the tension in the air.

"We are here with a purpose," Rohan whispered. "Let's act as though no one is following us. I feel sad about Mira and how time has passed without any real progress."

"You are right, Rohan; let's focus."

Passing by the *Tiergarten*, Rohan felt like withered autumn leaves the wind had carried away, forcibly thrown in a certain direction. He saw a tiny development toward getting nearer to the manuscript. Hopefully, meeting Fuchs would bring him closer to his mission.

The taxi took off at top speed on the motorway. With an exit at Halensee Street, the driver went straight to the villa in Grunewald. The weather had turned dull and cloudy, with no sunshine.

Priya and Rohan walked towards the pink-coloured villa. Droplets of an earlier rain looked like crystals on the outdoor furniture in the garden. The ponytailed man stopped his car at a distance, watching them. He did not get out of his car.

Rohan rang the doorbell. A middle-aged woman dressed like a nurse opened the door. Without asking them who they were, she led them in. The hall, with its shining marble floor, had an illuminated chandelier. They followed the woman upstairs. The elegant handrail was made of metal and wood. On the first floor, the living room had large windows with curtains moved to their sides.

The woman signalled them to sit on a leather sofa. In one corner stood a wooden table with several drawers. On top of it was a huge mirror. An elegant porcelain vase added some flavour to the room.

After a while, a man walked in. His wrinkles and his shrunken body showed his age. Fuchs smiled at his guests.

"I am Rohan Sharma. I spoke to you over the phone. This is my colleague, Priya Das."

"Nice to meet you." Fuchs shook hands with Priya and then Rohan. Joachim Fuchs sat on the sofa, his hand on his chin, ready to listen. "What have you discovered in Lanka?"

"We found a cylindrical shaped object," Rohan replied, "as

big as a helicopter, in the Indian Ocean. We have also found a notebook in a rice field. It belonged to Mr Shivkar Talpade, an aeronautical engineer and pilot, born in Maharashtra, India. Talpade's notebook proves that he died in his aircraft in 1900. Carbon tests have confirmed that the flying object belongs to the same time. It was three years before the Wright Brothers invented their flying machines."

"You mentioned a manuscript during our phone conversation," Fuchs inquired.

"We have also found a coffer," Rohan explained. "It looks like a small-sized treasure box; we believe there was a manuscript inside, probably the original version of the Vaimanika Shastra. We do not know where the original manuscript is."

"Vaimanika Shastra," Fuchs repeated, scratching his head. "The science of flying. I have dedicated my life to studying Indology, Mr Sharma. I would love to look at these wonderful artefacts of the flying machine. I am too old to travel to Lanka. Do you have their pictures with you?"

"Yes, here they are." Rohan opened his rucksack, pulled out photos of the flying machine, and gave them to Joachim Fuchs.

Fuchs wore his glasses and looked at the photos. "Amazing! I wish I had more energy to do what you are doing, to rediscover Asian history. My eyes are weak. I cannot see as I used to before. What do you want from me?"

"Our archaeological department believes that the Vaimanika Shastra must be here in Germany," Priya added. "We need your help to find it."

"Why do you think the manuscript is in Germany?" Fuchs inquired.

"We believe that German anthropologist Egon von Eickstedt, after his South Asian expedition, brought the manuscript with him to Germany. If my guess is right, he must have given it to Theodor Mollison, his sponsor." Priya responded.

Fuchs sat back, thought for a while and said, "Do you know what the manuscript looks like?"

"Probably, it has a wooden cover on the front and back," Priya explained. "The pages, I think, are made of palm leaves, loosely tied with a string, holding them together through two holes. The letters are usually exceptionally fine, scribed using a stylus and rubbed with lampblack. It should be around five centimetres high and twenty centimetres wide."

"It was during the mournful days of the Second World War," Fuchs began, "a shameful time where culture and civilisation were put to death for selfish reasons." Fuchs paused and thought for a while again. "It was during this period that a manuscript fell into the wrong hands, causing potent knowledge to slip away from safety. In a sense, this script shaped Hitler's persona, transforming him into a figure of great power."

"Did you know Egon von Eickstedt?" Priya inquired.

"I didn't know him personally," Fuchs replied, "but I remember it was during the reign of the Nazis. I was a young apprentice. I worked as an assistant to Theodor Mollison, an anthropologist at the University of Munich. Mollison was kindhearted and friendly; that was how he initially seemed.

"Egon von Eickstedt did not get any manuscript with him, but he only brought the information about the existence of a manuscript that held secret information about the art of flying. He gave this news to his friend, Theodor Mollison. Heinrich Himmler, a trusted confidant of Hitler, conceived the notion of conducting research into the history of the Aryan race.

"Himmler was the new leader of the political party NSDAP. The idea of building an Aryan nation became more potent than ever. In 1935, Himmler founded the *Ahnenerbe*, whose goal was to research the anthropological and cultural history of Southern Asia.

"They say evil is never satisfied until destruction is complete. Himmler intended to experiment and launch voyages to prove the Aryan supremacy in the ancient society of South Asia."

"The Nazis," Fuchs continued, "engaged many anthropologists, archaeologists and Indologists who obeyed their orders. Himmler glorified the Aryan race—his idea was to build a new Europe using old concepts.

"He wanted to promote Hitler as the next avatar of Vishnu, the one who had come down to earth to re-establish a new world order. Often, Himmler had a copy of the Bhagavad Gita in his hand. Once, I had heard him narrate the famous lines from the Gita:

यदा यदा हि धर्मस्य ग्लानिर्भवति भारत |
अभ्युत्थानमधर्मस्य तदात्मानं सृजाम्यहम् || ४ ७ ||

परित्राणाय साधूनां विनाशाय च दुष्कृताम् |
धर्मसंस्थापनार्थाय संभवामि युगे युगे || ४ ८ ||

yadā yadā hi dharmasya glānirbhavati bhārata
abhyutthānamadharmasya tadātmānaṃ sṛjāmyaham
paritrāṇāya sādhūnāṃ vināśāya ca duṣkṛtām
dharmasaṃsthāpanārthāya sambhavāmi yuge yuge

When there is disturbance or external intervention to the principles and laws of the universe,
I show Myself as the Power of eternal balancing.
To protect those in harmony and extinct the miscreants,
I incarnate Myself at every contingency of time.

"Those beautiful lines from the Bhagavad Gita are from Chapter 4, Hymns 7 and 8. It was too late when I realised that Himmler misused the message of Lord Krishna to the advantage of the Nazis. It haunted me for an exceptionally long time."

"When they learned that there were manuscripts with secret knowledge hidden in South Asia, the urge to find the manuscript on aeronautical science became intense.

"I got an opportunity to make more money. I accepted the offer; it helped me finance my studies. Himmler sponsored the first expedition to India. He sent scientists to find traces of the Aryan race. During those days, the British had a firm grip on India. Nevertheless, the Nazis somehow managed to enter the British territory. Ernst Schaefer, who led the expedition, first went to Calcutta."

"Why Ernst Schaefer? Why not Egon von Eickstedt?" Rohan inquired.

"Eickstedt opposed the Nazis and lost his job. He had never imagined that the Nazis would misuse his anthropological studies on the Asian race. Ernst Schaefer took Eickstedt's position. To conduct the risky task assigned to Schaefer, he mostly travelled by train.

"My job was to note down every message he sent to Germany. Sometimes, I also had to research to find the meaning of specific words and symbols in his letters. Schaefer discovered the Mahakala, the War God, whose symbol was a skull, which later became the symbol of the *Totenkopfstaffel*, a special unit of the SS.

"In Lanka, he met a powerful man from the Asura clan. In his message, Schaefer described the Asuras as warriors and said that they worshipped their ancestor Ravana, who they believed would protect them from all evil."

Fuchs paused for a while and spoke again, "Schaefer convinced the Asuras to rebel against the British rule. The Asuras entered into a treaty with Hitler. Hitler had promised the Asuras to defeat the British, give Lanka back to them and resurrect Ravana."

"A political allegiance between Hitler and the Asuras. Was that how it was?" Rohan inquired.

"Yes. Later, I realised that the Nazis were searching for the manuscript on the aeronautical science, the Vaimanika Shastra. Schaeffer had clearly discovered some information.

"Schaefer developed a solid plan—once he had found the original manuscript, he would replace it with a fake one, so the chief of the Asura would not at once realise about the missing manuscript. He stole the manuscript from the chief of the Asura."

"How did you know about the fake manuscript, Mr Fuchs?" Priya asked.

"I was the one who wrote it. I had to follow the orders of the Nazis."

"Where can I find the original manuscript?" Rohan asked.

Joachim Fuchs looked at his watch. "I didn't realise that the time has moved so quickly today. I am late for my lunch. Last week, I had a bad flu. My doctor has recommended that I eat on time and relax as much as possible. You will have to excuse me now."

"I must find that manuscript, Mr Fuchs. The chief of the Asura has abducted my wife, and only by finding the manuscript will she agree to release my wife."

"I am sorry about your wife, Mr Sharma." Fuchs sat back. "Why didn't you tell me before? Can you come back tomorrow afternoon? I need some time to think and remember."

After bidding farewell to Fuchs, Rohan and Priya stepped out of the house and onto the pavement. They scanned the surroundings but saw no sign of the man with the ponytail—no trace of his presence remained. Once seated in the taxi, they were driven back to their hotel. The man's absence now carried an air of mystery.

Chapter 20
Beyond the Nazis

The Seen, and that which Secret flies.
The weapon of the thousand eyes.
Ten-headed and the Hundred-faced,
Stargazer and the Layer-waste:
The Omen-bird, the Pure-from-spot,
The pair that wake and slumber not:

—Valmiki Ramayana, Book I, Canto XXX

"You've arrived punctually," Fuchs greeted them with a smile, appearing more at ease than the previous day. "I appreciate people who value time. Our conversation from yesterday brought me back to bygone days. In fact, discussing my past alleviates the burden I have carried for countless years."

"Why is your past a burden to you?" Rohan inquired eagerly.

"I suppose you haven't experienced war, so you may not fully understand the impact of witnessing such a thing. It has left a permanent scar on my mind, haunting me with memories too often." Fuchs paused before continuing, "Allow me to pick up where I left off yesterday.

"After Schaeffer brought the Vaimanika Shastra to Germany, he sought an Indologist named Walther Wuest to study the manuscript. One day, I overheard Wuest mention that it was an original Sanskrit work and that he had devoted countless hours to reading and deciphering its intricacies. As you may be aware, Sanskrit is a complex language, and only an expert can grasp the true meaning of its words.

"Wuest frequently visited Mollison to discuss the manuscript's contents, and I would sit near Mollison's door, occasionally catching snippets of their discussions. Wuest appeared enthralled by the discoveries he had made. The manuscript held a profound secret unknown to the world."

"Several days later, Wuest received a promotion, becoming the youngest professor at the University of Munich. He was also appointed Himmler's interpreter, tasked with translating the manuscript into German. I was responsible for meticulously recording every word he said."

"Was it the Vaimanika Shastra?" Rohan asked, seeking confirmation.

"It was the Vaimanika Shastra. The manuscript held tremendous influence over the Nazis. It provided them with what they desired: the ability to launch aerial attacks against their enemies. The repercussions of the Lankan expedition, along with the manuscript and its concepts, found their way from South Asia to the Nazis and their V-rocket program. Eventually, these ideas became intertwined with Project Paperclip and NASA's moon rocket program. I apologise for overwhelming you with abundant information all at once."

"Please tell us everything you know," Rohan pleaded, realising the necessity of gathering as much information as possible. "Otherwise, it will be exceedingly difficult to uncover the truth."

Fuchs began recounting, "In 1937, the Nazis initiated their rocket program. They established a scientific research and development site in Peenemuende, located near the island of Ruegen in northern Germany. During that period, various countries were experimenting with rockets. However, none achieved substantial success.

"The Germans faced significant challenges in constructing

stable rockets and struggled to attain controlled movement. Mollison once mentioned to me that the Vaimanika Shastra was present in Peenemuende. The rocket program officially commenced in 1941, leading to the development of the V1 and V2 rockets.

"The V2, a massive machine capable of carrying explosives weighing up to one ton, achieved a significant milestone in 1944 when it became the first human-made object to leave Earth's atmosphere. The Nazis achieved what had confounded other nations, leaving the rest of the world astonished."

Fuchs continued, "I've heard that the Vaimanika Shastra contributed to their understanding of flight principles, particularly the challenges of maintaining controlled flight within the atmosphere. However, I can't offer more details since I am not a scientist.

"Wernher von Braun led this project. He was driven by ambition and aspired to reach the moon one day. Germany's defeat in the war was followed by the collapse of the *Deutsche Reich*. The research and development site in Peenemuende near the Polish border led the rocket scientists to flee to Bavaria to evade the advancing Russians.

"They hoped that the Americans would rescue them. For several weeks, the scientists resided in a hotel in Bavaria before Von Braun initiated negotiations with the Americans. They later went to Los Alamos and White Sands in the United States. Eventually, Wernher von Braun and many others joined forces to set up NASA."

Fuchs leaned back in his chair, closing his eyes for a moment, seemingly lost in contemplation or recollecting past events.

"Do you think the rocket scientists may have taken the manuscript to the United States?" Rohan inquired.

"I cannot say for certain whether they did, but I do know that in 1945, before Germany's collapse, the Nazis were believed to have transported valuable possessions to a secure location in the hopes of one-day reclaiming power. They were hiding near Lake Toplitz in Austria."

"Where do you think the manuscript might be today?" Rohan leaned in.

Fuchs sighed, his gaze distant as he recalled the past, "Those were harrowing times for me as a young apprentice. I only saw the original manuscript once, in a Nazi bunker, where it was securely locked away. After that, I've never seen it.

"Towards the end of the Second World War, Mollison destroyed all the translation work we had painstakingly undertaken. I can't say if the Vaimanika Shastra met the same fate, whether it was consigned to the flames.

"I had taken an oath to remain silent about its existence. I have shared with you everything I knew. I sincerely hope that you find your wife soon."

Rohan and Priya extended their hands to bid farewell.

Priya, sensing Rohan's melancholic silence, attempted to break the tension. "How about going out for dinner tonight? I know a nice restaurant," she suggested, hoping to lift his spirit. Rohan looked at her momentarily. "I am hungry. Let's go then," he responded, standing up, ready to accompany her.

Walking towards Berlin's *Gendarmenmarkt* that evening, the city appeared inviting despite the threatening grey sky hinting at more rain. Rohan, under the shelter of his hat, closed his eyes, relishing the purity of the crisp air with each breath.

They passed by notable sights such as the statue of poet Friedrich Schiller, the German cathedral, and the concert hall. A young man adorned with long hair and a poncho sat on the steps at the concert hall entrance, skilfully playing melodies on his flute. Rohan listened to the enchanting music, allowing his gaze to wander across the surroundings he found so beautiful.

Suddenly, rain began to drizzle down upon them. Seeking refuge, they hurriedly entered a narrow street and settled in the restaurant, sitting near a window. Once their orders were placed, Rohan drew closer to the misted panes, his breath fogging them slightly. He peered through the window, fixating on the shop opposite their table.

Inside, a collection of dolls dressed in romantic garments—gloves, shawls, and coats—stared back at him with motionless eyes set in pale wax faces as if silently observing the events unfolding around them. At that moment, Rohan felt like those dolls—still and powerless.

After dinner, they stepped out of the restaurant. The rain had subsided. Rohan's gaze fell upon a figure standing at the street corner. His words caught in his throat as he watched the man tilt his chin upward, his narrowed eyes gleaming unusually. Pointing towards him, Rohan alerted Priya, "That man—the one with the ponytail and beard—he's here again, following us."

Priya stared at the man, trying to recognise him. "Who could he possibly be?"

Rohan felt a dryness in his mouth, and a knot of discomfort formed in his stomach as they approached the corner where the man stood. In tension, the man locked eyes with Rohan and Priya, adjusted his collar, and swiftly departed, walking away briskly into the labyrinthine network of backstreets. Determined to unravel the mystery, they searched, wandering through the area for a while, scanning their surroundings, but their efforts proved fruitless in locating the mysterious man.

"Who is he? Why is he following us?" Priya remarked.

"Did you see how quickly he left when he noticed us approaching?" Rohan said. "Never did I imagine that one day, my wife would be kidnapped in Lanka, and here I am, wandering the streets of Berlin, suspecting every passer-by. It's driving me to the brink of madness."

"Anyone in your position would feel the same, Rohan."

"If something were to happen to Mira, my life would lose all meaning. I can't bear the thought." He rubbed his eyes, a fog of uncertainty settling upon him.

"Don't say that, Rohan. We have to maintain a positive mindset," Priya urged.

"You're right, Priya. We must remain optimistic. Don't you think that the man who was following us had the opportunity to harm us? But it appears he's biding his time. Someone seems to know what we're up to, but we are still clueless about their motives. We have to be vigilant because he could strike at any moment. We can't let the search of the manuscript come to a dead end." Rohan had a sense of urgency in his tone.

"It's such a peculiar situation we find ourselves in. We've already gathered quite some knowledge about the manuscript," Rohan continued, taking out a cigarette and placing it in his mouth.

Priya frowned. "I don't understand what makes smoking so appealing."

"Would you like to give it a try?"

"No, I can't afford to add any extra strain to my life."

The dense fog began to rise, casting an ethereal atmosphere; Rohan noticed a black BMW parked across the street, its sleek form illuminated by the warm yellow glow of the street lamps. Through the mist, he saw two shadowy figures inside the car. Could one of them be the man who had been tailing them? It wasn't easy to say. Lately, it seemed as though Rohan had encountered far too many people interested in the manuscript.

"What should we do now?" Priya inquired, her voice tinged with concern.

"Let's head to the train station and secure reservations for tomorrow to Leipzig," he suggested.

Later that evening, at Rohan's request, Priya made another call to Arthur Hoffmann. "He's not available," she reported after the conversation. "His secretary mentioned that Hoffmann has postponed his return, and she couldn't provide an exact date for when he would return from his trip abroad."

"I have a peculiar feeling that we're wasting our time trying to reach him," he said.

Chapter 21
Leipzig

> The rising sun with golden rays,
> Light of the worlds, adore and praise:
> The universal king, the lord
> By hosts of heaven and fiends adored.
>
> —Valmiki Ramayana, Book VI, Canto CVI

The train station in Leipzig had a huge platform area and with its combination of glass and steel, it looked like an oversized cathedral. Priya and Rohan left the train station and crossed a busy street that led them into the old city quarter.

Walking along the park and into the *Goethestrasse*, they passed by a small lake. The old buildings from the communist era were in a frenzy of transformation, giving way to new, ubiquitous urban structures. At *Augustusplatz*, the Krochhaus Tower stood tall and was adorned with a chiming bell reminiscent of the famous *Torre dell'Orologio* in Venice. The words *Omnio vincit labor* were inscribed on the tower, serving as a reminder that hard work conquers all.

The Grassi Museum's collection showcased the immense wealth accumulated by generations of Leipzig merchants, fondly nicknamed the *Pfeffersaecke*, pepper sacks or money bags, symbolising the city's pride and heritage. Despite meticulously examining all the artefacts from Lanka, Rohan was disappointed to realise that the manuscript he sought was nowhere to be found.

"Let me speak to the manager," Priya suggested, heading towards the office. Rohan followed her. They approached the manager's office, where the name Arnold Herrscher was displayed. The man seated at the desk appeared to be in his forties. As Priya explained the situation, Herrscher's face flushed, clouded with deep thought.

"I have a crucial meeting I can't afford to miss. Could you meet me here tomorrow at noon?" he suggested, his voice hinting firmness in his accent.

"I believe he might have some information for us," Rohan speculated as they exited the museum.

It was a bright sunny day as Rohan prepared himself for what he hoped would be a fruitful visit to the Grassi Museum in Leipzig. To his surprise, Arnold Herrscher, the person he intended to meet, was absent from his desk, and the receptionist did not know his whereabouts. Rohan and Priya waited outside Herrscher's office, hoping he would come any moment.

Even after an hour, there was no sign of him. Rohan suspected that Herrscher was playing some game. A middle-aged woman approached them and asked, "*Sind Sie Priya Das und Rohan Sharma?*" (Are you Priya Das and Rohan Sharma?)

"Yes," Priya replied.

The woman handed them an envelope and expressed Herrscher's apologies for being unable to meet them.

"Arnold Herrscher has left us a note," Priya announced, opening the envelope. "He wants us to meet him at 2 pm at the Mephisto Bar in *Auerbachs Keller*, located at the Maedler passage."

"I knew it!" Rohan exclaimed, rising from his seat. "This man must have valuable information. And if we're fortunate, he might even have the manuscript with him."

"I can't help but feel something is amiss. Why does he want to meet at the Maedler passage instead of the museum?" Priya voiced her concerns.

"We'll have to wait and find out," Rohan replied.

They arrived at Auerbachs Keller in the Maedler passage ahead of Herrscher's designated time. The passage, bustling with tourists, was adorned with jewellery stores, shoe boutiques, and other designer shops. Rohan and Priya took their seats at the Mephisto Bar, awaiting Arnold Herrscher's arrival. In silence, they raised their glasses, exchanging glances that hinted at their shared connection as if they were members of a secret society.

"You know, Rohan, this restaurant has a rich history dating back to the fifteenth century," Priya remarked.

"It's incredible how well-preserved it is," Rohan observed, scanning the surroundings.

"By the sixteenth century, it had already gained prominence as one of the city's most renowned wine bars. It even features in Johann Wolfgang von Goethe's play *Faust*, as the place where Mephistopheles introduces Faust to their fateful journey. It's said that Goethe frequented this place during his studies in Leipzig," Priya shared.

"That's fascinating," Rohan remarked, his gaze wandering around the bar as if he could sense the lingering presence of Mephistopheles. The bar, built in 1438, showcased three paintings on its walls, all dated 1625. One depicted Mephistopheles enticing Faust on a transformative journey, while the second portrayed the magician and astrologer Faust enjoying drinks with students. In the third painting, Faust gallantly rode out the door with his legs wrapped around a wine barrel.

"It does feel like we've made a pact with the devil ourselves, although in our case, the devil could be either Herrscher, the museum chief, or Kali, the chief of the Asuras. I'm not entirely certain," Rohan mused, glancing at his watch. "Herrscher is running late."

Just as they were discussing, Herrscher entered the bar with a tense expression. He spoke rapidly in German, leaving Rohan unable to comprehend his words.

"He says," Priya translated, "that he can help us locate the manuscript. He knows where it is."

"Where is it?" Rohan asked, his voice filled with restlessness.

"He's asking for money," Priya conveyed.

"How much?" Rohan inquired.

"Five thousand euros in cash," Herrscher replied.

"What? That's too much. How about two?" Rohan tried to negotiate.

"You give me five or forget about the manuscript," Herrscher insisted firmly.

"We'll need some time to arrange the money," Priya explained. "Can we have your phone number?"

"Sorry, no phone number. I'll meet you here tomorrow. Get the money." Herrscher swiftly left the bar.

That night in Berlin, sleep eluded Rohan. Thoughts of the manuscript consumed his mind. He realised that obtaining the required cash within two days would be daunting. The only potential source of financial assistance in Germany was Priya. He wondered if she would be able to secure the money in time.

The following morning, Rohan sat alone at the breakfast table, and Priya was absent. A waiter approached Rohan and handed him a note. He read the message: *I will meet you at 8:30 in the hotel lobby with the money. Priya.*

Relief washed over Rohan's face. She would get the cash. What if Arnold Herrscher deceived them? What if he didn't have the manuscript after all? There was no guarantee. Anxiously awaiting Priya's return in the lobby, Rohan's tension mounted. The clock ticked half-past eight, and she was not there.

Had something happened to her? Why did she go alone? Why hadn't she taken him along? Finally, he spotted her entering the lobby, a bag slung over her shoulder.

"We need to hurry; the train to Leipzig departs in about twenty minutes. Let's take a taxi!" Priya said, her voice filled with urgency.

"Do you have the money?"

"Yes, I do."

"Thank you. I will repay you as soon as I can."

"It's alright, Rohan. Let's focus on finding the manuscript first."

"I'm so glad you're here with me."

"Don't worry, Rohan. We'll get through this."

In Leipzig, they rushed to the Mephisto Bar in Auerbach's cellar, where Herrscher was already waiting. Sweat glistened on his forehead. He asked, "Do you have the money?"

"I'd like to see the manuscript first," Rohan insisted.

"You don't trust me?" Herrscher retorted. "No money, no manuscript."

Priya handed him a packet wrapped in brown paper. Herrscher opened it and inspected its content. Then, he handed over a piece of paper and swiftly left.

"Hey! Wait!" Rohan called out, but Herrscher was already gone.

"Someone named Anton Gartenberger has the manuscript," Priya read from the note Herrscher gave her. "Here is his address in Vienna. What if the address turns out to be incorrect?"

"If the address is wrong, at least we know where Herrscher works. We can always come back," Rohan reassured her. "Did you notice the tattoo on his arm?"

"No. What was it?"

"It was a black sun. He's a neo-Nazi. He's betraying his community by giving us the information about the manuscript."

"I think he needed money. I wonder what the black sun symbolises," Priya pondered.

"The neo-Nazis use the black sun as their symbol, although the Nazis used the swastika. They believe the black sun is a mystical source of energy that can rejuvenate the Aryan race. The black sun is depicted as a circular ring with twelve spokes emanating from its centre, resembling the symbol of the *Schutzstaffel* or SS. It also represents the invisible sun, the anti-sun, or the shadow of the invisible spiritual light. The material fire is seen as the shadow of the spiritual light," Rohan explained.

"Come on, Rohan. Let's go. I have a strong feeling that we're being watched," Priya urged. They quickly made their way out of Auerbach's cellar.

Chapter 22
Vienna

> Sore wounded by the shaft that came
> With lightning speed and surest aim,
> Blood spouting from her mouth and side.
> She fell upon the earth and died.
> —Valmiki Ramayana, Book I, Canto XXVIII

On the flight from Berlin, Rohan reflected on the extraordinary events of the past few weeks, which made ordinary stories seem insignificant by comparison. Anton Gartenberger, a prominent figure working for the United Nations in Vienna's nuclear test program, held considerable influence—something Rohan had uncovered through a quick online search.

The journey to Vienna was brief, just an hour and a half. Upon landing, they took a taxi to a hotel near the State Opera.

After taking a moment to freshen up, Rohan and Priya went ahead to the address provided by Arnold Herrscher. Located on the ring road encircling the historic city, atop Café Prueckel stood Anton Gartenberger's penthouse. Its prime location was in the striking neighbourhood of the city park and the Museum of Modern Art.

Rohan stood near the entrance of the building, waiting for someone to open the door and let him in. His attention shifted to a crow perched on a nearby tree, cawing loudly. It circled closer, flying in loops above him. Could it be an Asura tracking him? Watching his every move? Suddenly, with a swift swoop, the crow descended, landing on the ground before him. Its eyes seemed to hold a message. As it took off and flew away, he couldn't shake the feeling that this encounter might have a deeper significance beyond mere coincidence.

Priya stood at a distance, observing the five-story building. Grey skies and autumn winds signalled the approaching rain. After some time, an elderly woman stepped out of the building, a dog by her side. Seizing the opportunity, Rohan moved to enter, but the woman's questioning gaze stopped him in his tracks.

"*Sie wohnen hier nicht, oder?*" (You don't live here, do you?) she asked, her tone suspicious.

"I'm visiting a friend," he lied, hoping to avoid further questions and gain entry.

Once inside, he ascended the stairs with the quiet grace of a cat. Moving cautiously down the corridor, his rubber-soled shoes muffled each step, ensuring he remained unnoticed.

The foyer was adorned with ornate arches set against vibrant tiles, creating an atmosphere of old-world charm. Though motion-sensor lights flickered on as he moved, the space was eerily empty. He continued deeper into the building until he reached the apartment, feeling one step closer to uncovering the mysteries ahead.

From a small leather case in his rucksack, he retrieved a tool with a curved end, typically used for prying open boxes at archaeological sites. After a few attempts with a set of adaptable keys, he unlocked the door and stepped in cautiously.

The interior was modern and luxurious. The television was on as he walked along the wall. In the circle of yellow light thrown by the chandelier, he saw someone dressed in a sports suit sitting in a relaxed manner on a leather sofa. He stopped and became cautious. When he noticed that the man did not move, he carefully walked towards him and saw his eyes closed, realising that he was sleeping on the sofa. There was no one else in the apartment.

Anton Gartenberger must be around fifty years old, he guessed. When he took a closer look at the man, he noticed a tattoo on his hand, a black sun, like the one he had seen on the museum manager in Leipzig.

The shelf against the wall was artfully arranged and full of books. Gartenberger was undoubtedly a book collector. In the adjoining room, with windows on the angled roof, was a glass cupboard with antique books, one of them wrapped in a red silk cloth. He unlocked the glass door, took the book in his hand, and opened it. It was an ancient manuscript with a title scribed on the wooden bound, the Vaimanika Shastra.

He stood, rejoicing momentarily with his eyes fixed on the ancient script. Then he opened his rucksack, put the manuscript in it, left the apartment, took the elevator and quickly left the building. Noticing him come out, Priya stood up from the wooden bench. "Let's go," he said to Priya, walking quickly.

"Did you get it?" she asked.

"Yes," he answered. They quickly walked towards the Café Prueckel. "Just imagine, I have the original version of Vaimanika Shastra in my bag. Oh! I can't wait for Mira's release. If I have ever got a chance, I would read it and decipher the ancient script."

A taxi stood across the street. They waited at the restaurant's corner to cross the street with heavy traffic. When the pedestrian signal turned green, Priya started walking across the street. At that moment, Rohan's phone rang. Still standing on the pavement, he picked up the phone from his pocket.

When he looked up, he saw that Priya was already in the middle of the street. Suddenly, a heavy truck came swinging into the road, smashing the flowerpots at the junction. Then the truck swerved sharply away from the Café and roared along the street towards Priya.

The massive tyres loomed up over her. The truck struck Priya full-on and drove her off her feet and into the air, throwing her into the street itself. She landed hard on her face, broken and bleeding.

Rohan screamed from the pavement, protesting. The reckless driver swerved at that moment, steering the thick tyres straight towards her as the truck lurched back onto the street. The tyres rolled fully over her, then accelerated rapidly, and the truck raced off. By the time Rohan realised what had happened, the truck had vanished from the site. Rohan rushed to Priya. She lay still, not breathing at all.

Rohan screamed, "Please, someone call the ambulance." The suddenness and fright paralysed Rohan.

The police concluded Priya's death was an accident. However, from what Rohan had seen with his own eyes, it appeared quite different. In his view, it was murder with deliberation. When the truck had turned on the street, it had been going too slowly to be out of control. What's more, the driver had ignored the red light.

When the driver struck her the first time, it seemed as if he had aimed at her. Picking up speed, when he swung back a second time, the driver must have been able to see Priya and could have avoided hitting her the second time. Instead, he had aimed straight at Priya, crushing her again, and had driven away even faster, in full control of his vehicle.

Rohan could not prove that this was a deliberate act of a hit-and-run case. He did not voice his suspicions to the police.

He had no evidence that this might have been a murder. If he expressed his doubts, the police would not believe him, so he remained silent.

It was inconceivable; Priya was the mildest, sweetest person and an excellent scholar. Why would someone want to kill her in this foreign country? What could have been the motive? The next thing that came to his mind was the manuscript. Then, he realised he had lost his rucksack.

He searched around the hospital, in the lobby, at the entrance, at the gate, and in the ambulance parked outside. He asked people around, but the rucksack was gone, and along with it, he had lost the manuscript. He tried to recall what had happened. Having seen the accident from a close distance, he had been in a state of shock.

But before that, when he had received the phone call, he had held his rucksack in his right hand. Suddenly, he remembered seeing the man with a beard and ponytail, the same person he had seen in the library. He had followed them in Berlin when he had gone out for dinner with Priya. This man had been present at the accident scene.

Rohan recalled how the man had stood close to him, and at that time, he had no bag. Later, at the arrival of the ambulance, Rohan saw the same person walking away with a rucksack in his hand. Now, he realised that it must have been his rucksack. He felt devastated; his mouth was dry, and he felt uncomfortable in his stomach.

The police officer in Vienna was warm and caring. After Rohan's identity was clear, the police officer explained, "The description of the truck given by all those who eye-witnessed the scene varied, probably because of the confusion, but efforts are being made to find the truck. This case has turned out to be a little complicated. Honestly, I cannot assure you how long it will take to find his whereabouts."

Although he was still in shock, Rohan's rational mind kicked in, and he had to find Priya's parents' address. The police officer cooperated in sending Priya's body to her parents.

Rohan had no idea what he should do next. He had already lost so much time searching for the manuscript that he could not afford to waste more time. He decided to return to Lanka without the manuscript in search of Mira. He hoped that Inspector Chris would help him find her.

He realised that Inspector Chris had called him when the accident happened. After Priya's misfortune and untimely death, Rohan forgot to call Chris back. He picked up his mobile phone to dial his number, but the phone's battery was completely low. He went to his hotel room, packed his things, took a taxi, and went straight to the airport.

Chapter 23
Back to Lanka

> From house to house, he hurried on,
> And the wild flames behind him shone.
> Each mansion of the foe he scaled,
> And furious fire, its roof assailed
> Till all the common ruin shared.
>
> —Valmiki Ramayana, Book V, Canto LIV

It was terrible, thought Inspector Chris, how little progress they had made, how tiny the collection of circumstantial evidence on the series of murders was. The recurring question that troubled him was where he could find a lead to the murderer's identity. If Kali, the chief of the Asuras, was indeed responsible, he wondered why she had chosen to abduct Mira instead of outright killing her, just as she allegedly had killed the others.

Reflecting on the abduction of Mira, Chris believed it had been executed flawlessly. Kali seemed confident that law enforcement couldn't establish any convicting proof against her.

"Please update me on your progress," Inspector Chris inquired Constable Vijaya.

"Sir, you had tasked me to gather information about Arthur Hoffmann. We've just received news that Hoffmann has returned to Lanka."

"Where is he currently?"

"We're still trying to locate him, sir."

"Didn't you arrange for the airport authorities to inform us upon his arrival? How could this have gone unnoticed?"

"He did not fly in, sir. He had entered Lanka through the port from India."

"We had also informed the port authorities, hadn't we?"

"Yes, sir, but they claim not to have recognised him and didn't inform us."

"And how do we know that Hoffmann is in Lanka?"

"A taxi driver has said he dropped Hoffmann near Adam's Peak."

"That sounds interesting." Chris stroked his unshaven chin. "The Asura village is close to Adam's Peak. It's in the forest, and we need to search. Let's go!"

They undertook a lengthy drive towards the forest before finally arriving where they could park. They continued on foot, navigating the vast expanse of the central highland. Throughout the walk, Inspector Chris maintained an unwavering silence, his thoughts consumed by the weighty task ahead.

Constable Vijaya dutifully followed the lead of his superior. After a while, they paused to rest beneath the shade of a tree.

Sensing the need for a momentary break, he retrieved a flask of alcohol from his pocket. Settling himself upon a nearby rock, he took a swig, allowing the bitter liquid to course through his veins.

"Sir, may I speak?" the constable inquired.

"You don't need to seek my permission. Just go ahead," replied the officer.

"Sir, you drink too much. Even on duty. It's not good for your health."

"Vijaya, this is my only way to cope with the stress that comes with this job."

"What about your family? Your wife?"

"I had a wife once. We're divorced now. I don't blame her for that."

"I am sorry to hear that, sir."

"Don't be sorry, Vijaya. She left because she couldn't handle the strain I suffered as a police officer. We need to suppress our emotions to keep going. My mind has developed a defence mechanism so I can function in difficult circumstances. If I maintained my natural sensitivity, I'd fall apart. My ex-wife couldn't handle it. Since we split, others' pain doesn't affect me, and I've become indifferent to hurting others. Are you married?"

"No, sir."

"Girlfriend?"

"Yes, sir."

"Here's my advice; take good care of her. She deserves it."

"Thank you for the advice, sir."

"Don't move," Chris cautioned abruptly. Constable Vijaya froze in his place, feeling uneasy. "It must have rained here last night. The ground appears damp enough to retain footprints."

He tracked the path, studying it closely. Two distinct sets of footprints from two different pairs of shoes were clearly visible. The soft earth displayed a discernible trail. The imprints on the right were deeper than those on the left. One person seemed heavier than the other.

They stumbled upon drops of blood that had fallen onto the ground. A bit farther along, Chris spotted two men: one seated beneath a tree, the other standing. Chris went on high alert. Storing his alcohol flask, he retrieved his gun and positioned himself behind a tree. Vijaya mimicked his actions, taking cover behind another tree.

Recognising the uniformed officers, one of the men commented, "Ah, police. Why do the police always arrive so late? I'm a victim here, officer. The villain is long gone. You're late."

"Arthur Hoffmann, how can I trust your words?" Inspector

Chris emerged behind the tree, putting his gun back in its holster.

"This is my friend, Peter Herbert," Hoffmann said, pointing at the man beside him. "He saved my life today."

Herbert, the bearded man with a long ponytail, retrieved a handkerchief from his pocket and used it to bind Hoffmann's injured hand.

"What happened, Hoffmann? Who did this to you?" Chris inquired.

"If you run in this direction." Hoffmann pointed to his right. "You'll find the man responsible for my condition."

"Tell me the details and who it was," prompted Chris.

"He was an Asura, officer. He would have killed me if Peter hadn't arrived just in time. I came here to find Kali. But before I could shoot her, the man, her bodyguard, seized my gun and tried to strike me down with his axe."

"Why did you intend to kill her?"

"To avenge the death of my friend, Professor Shastry."

"How are you sure Kali killed Professor Shastry?"

"I saw it. Sadly, Professor Shastry passed away before I could rescue him."

"Why do you think Kali killed Professor Shastry?"

"Kali, a descendant of Ravana, can't tolerate anyone who writes about her ancestor. That's why she kills the authors and severs their fingers."

"How do you know?"

"From that man with the axe. I want to see Kali either dead or behind bars. She also wanted to kill me, just as she did with Professor Shastry."

"I'd strangle that brute with my own hands if given the chance," Herbert added.

Chris directed his attention to the hefty axe lying on the

ground. Picking it up, he felt its sharp blade. He noticed a peacock emblem etched onto the haft. "Kali has left behind evidence. The peacock is the symbol of the Asuras," he remarked.

Herbert departed without further words, his manner suggesting a predetermined purpose as if Hoffmann and he had already plotted their next steps. Hoffmann rose, deep in thought. "The situation has taken a darker turn now," he said.

"I'm confused. Utterly confused," Chris admitted. "Let's assume, just for a moment, that Kali kills anyone who writes about Ravana. How would she even know who is writing about him?"

"She claims to hear the voice of Ravana," Hoffmann clarified. "It's this voice that compels her to kill; they say Ravana's words are remarkably clear. The Ramayana's epic tale has brought disgrace upon the Asuras. Despite being written thousands of years ago, they still suffer the consequences of being Ravana's descendants. It's as straightforward as that."

"It's a complete void," the inspector confessed. "So, the spirit of Ravana is guiding them to commit these murders?"

"That's what Kali claims," Hoffmann added.

Chris placed his alcohol flask in his mouth, took a thoughtful sip, and pondered, "How strange." He turned his gaze swiftly towards Hoffmann's direction, concerned that Hoffmann might be moving towards the Asura village.

"What's your plan, Hoffmann?" Chris inquired, signalling Vijaya to accompany them.

"We'll trek through the wilderness—the path leading to the Asura village," Hoffmann said, leading them across the plains towards the village.

Hoffmann gathered dry leaves and ignited them. Herbert returned, carrying large cans, from which he doused the trees along the village's ridge with kerosene. The fire caught up instantly.

Chris stood speechless. Hoffmann and Herbert collected more dry branches, lit them, and hurled them at the houses, which eventually succumbed to the flames.

"Stop!" Chris cried out. "Families live here—innocent women and children. Don't do this." His pleas were ignored. Panic soon engulfed the Asura households. Hoffmann continued to pour kerosene onto the forest while Herbert navigated the opposite side of the woods, leaving a trail of kerosene. Within minutes, the village and the surrounding forest were consumed by a raging inferno.

"Sir," Vijaya shook Chris, disbelief in his eyes. "Sir, we need to call for more help."

"You are right," Chris responded, retrieving his phone. However, there was no signal.

Chapter 24
Lanka is Burning

> Her pallid cheek, her tangled hair,
> Her raiment showed her deep despair,
> Near and more near the envoy came
> And gently hailed the weeping dame.
> She started up in sweet surprise,
> And sudden joy illumed her eyes.
>
> —Valmiki Ramayana, Book VI, Canto CXV

After a long day of agitated silence enforced by the death of Priya, who had been a close friend, and after losing the most valued manuscript, Rohan, pale as his linen suit, landed at Colombo airport. He took a taxi towards the forest, where he had met the Asuras, hoping Mira was still alive. The only thing he had in his mind was to find and rescue her. But how? He did not know.

Near the forest, he got out of the taxi and hiked the trail he had been on earlier. After a few hours of walking, he heard noises. He slowed his pace. The air hissed and moaned. The fire had seized the fragile forest. One tree after the other was burning, sending up tongues of flame.

"Put out that fire. Quick," Rohan heard someone cry. "Everything will burn up."

Thick smoke covered the village. Rohan rushed closer, unsure what to do. He was distressed, thinking about Mira. Was she there? The villagers poured water to smother the fire. The flames were so high that they consumed the vegetation and destroyed the warehouse.

Amid the dangerous confusion, Rohan saw Inspector Chris. In an explosion of anger, Chris violently pushed an old man, an Asura. The old man slammed into the outside wall of the hangar, banging his head against one corner, and fell to the ground. Someone in the crowd uttered a horrible curse, but Chris paid no heed to him.

Rohan turned to the hangar, which was utterly caught up by fire. Was there an ancient flying machine inside? Too late, he would never know. If there was one, then the remains must already be burning. The villagers carried loads of water from the nearby river. Rohan snatched a bucket and poured water over the hangar. It subdued only a ridiculously few flashes before the fire burst into a high flame again.

Realising he would not be able to put the fire out with his hands, Inspector Chris decided to save the forest by using wood. He seized logs of wood in the warehouse and used them as weapons to suppress the fire. He slammed and stirred the burning wood. More sparks rose and hovered in the air.

Chaos consumed the village as flames devoured the wooden structures, painting the blue sky with an ominous orange glow. Desperate villagers scrambled to save whatever they could, their cries of anguish and fear mingling with the relentless crackling of the fire. Amid the turmoil, the grand house of Kali, the Asura chief, stood firm and defiant—its sturdy walls now menaced by the approaching blaze.

"Rohan, follow me," Chris cried out.

Rohan and Inspector Chris went towards the big house that belonged to Kali. They braved the intensifying heat and entered the house in search of Mira, their hearts pounding with urgency. The air inside was thick with smoke, making it difficult to see. They coughed and choked as they called out for Mira, praying she was within reach.

Rohan combed each room through the billowing haze, frantically searching for any sign of his beloved wife. The crackling of fire grew louder, a cruel reminder of the encroaching danger. Time seemed to stretch, each passing moment heightening his anxiety.

And then, amidst the chaos, their voices echoing through the house, Chris heard a faint cry for help. "I hear some voice here, Rohan," he called.

Guided by the sound, Rohan and Chris pushed through the smoke-filled corridors until they discovered Mira trapped in a room, her face etched with fear. Rohan hurried to save her from the imminent danger.

"Are you okay?" Rohan shouted amidst the deafening roar from the village.

"What took you so long?" She held Rohan in her arms.

"I'm so sorry." He hugged her. "We need to get out of here."

Together, they navigated through the treacherous path back to safety, the heat intensifying with each step. The windows and the whole façade flickered with irregular flashes. The village outside continued to burn, the crackling flames hungrily devouring everything in their path.

Yet, Rohan, Chris, and Mira, against all odds, emerged from the house just as the fire's relentless grip tightened its hold on the place they had narrowly escaped. Gasping for air, their bodies covered in soot, Rohan stumbled into the arms of Mira, the weight of relief crashing upon him.

"Kali has escaped," announced Chris. "She has also taken some of her people with her."

"I am glad she didn't take Mira with her." Rohan smiled.

"I'm free," Mira rejoiced. "Thank you for saving my life, Inspector." She held Chris's hand.

"I'm only doing my job." Chris shrugged his shoulders. "I heard about Priya. I'm so sorry." He looked at Rohan. "Both the murders—Professor Shastry and Professor Karthigesu—were committed by Kali herself. We have an eyewitness and enough evidence to prove it."

Mira looked at Rohan. "What happened to Priya? I'd like to know the troubling events when we can catch our breath."

The wind had become furious again, violently spreading the fire. Sparks caught the manes of domesticated animals. The terrified animals broke their halters, kicked down the doors, scattered over the grounds, neighing, mooing, bleating, and grunting horribly.

By now, the fire had reached all the houses, blowing clouds of sparks into the air. The fire had caught everything in the village.

"Let's get out of here," Inspector Chris suggested. "Where would you like to go?" he inquired.

"We don't have a place yet; we need to find one," Rohan replied.

"How about Kalutara? There's a charming hotel I know of. If you're lucky, you might find a pleasant surprise there," Chris suggested.

"No more surprises, please," Mira said.

"If you run into any problems, call me," Chris said.

Chapter 25
Meeting Hoffmann

Then hadst thou shunned the fruitless strife
Nor jeopardised thy noble life,
But spared thy friends and bold allies
Their vain and weary enterprise.

—Valmiki Ramayana, Book VI, Canto CXVIII

"This place is breathtaking!" Mira exclaimed as she settled herself at the breakfast table in Kalutara.

"Did you manage to get some good sleep, my dear?" Rohan asked.

"For a little while," Mira replied. They sat together in the seaside garden, which was covered by towering trees, elegant bamboo, vibrant blossoms, crawling vines, and lush ferns. The sound of the rolling waves from the nearby Indian Ocean filled the air, and they watched the fishermen in the distance.

"I tried to book our flight back home, but no flights are available until Sunday. So, we'll have to spend some nights here," Rohan shared a tinge of disappointment in his voice.

"Don't worry about it, Rohan. Who wouldn't enjoy staying in this paradise? Just look at this marvellous view." Her finger extended towards the sunlit expanse, the vibrant greenery, and the crystal-clear blue sky.

"I thought you'd be eager to leave this country after everything happened."

"You know, Rohan. I've been thinking about it. I must let go of the past and move forward. Things could have turned out much worse for us. I'm still alive, and we're here together, enjoying this breakfast in such a beautiful location. It's not easy, but I must find a way to forgive those who kidnapped me and those who took my father's life. This country isn't to blame for what happened. I need to come to terms with reality."

"You're right, Mira. I want to help you find the peace you deserve."

"I can't wait to dive into the water. If you don't mind…"

"Go ahead. I'll join you in a little while," Rohan replied. She made her way towards the shoreline.

Arthur Hoffmann, the man whose name had reverberated in Rohan's ears countless times before, made his way into the garden, heading in his direction. He was tall, blond, with a distinctive nose.

A peculiar thought crossed Rohan's mind. Did Inspector Chris know that Hoffmann was here? Was that the reason he had suggested this particular hotel?

"Would you mind if I join you?" Hoffmann asked.

"Have a seat." Rohan gestured towards a chair. "I've been trying to come to terms with everything that has happened in the past few days. It hasn't been easy,"

Hoffmann sat in the chair opposite Rohan. "My condolences for the loss of Professor Shastry. I'm also deeply sorry about your wife's kidnapping."

"We're still alive," he remarked with a subtle wink. "I heard from Inspector Chris that you were a close friend of Professor Shastry," Rohan mentioned.

"Professor Shastry was a cherished friend, a remarkable person. I miss him dearly. I didn't know that he had such a wonderful daughter and a remarkable son-in-law," Hoffmann said. "As soon as I learnt about Shastry's daughter's abduction, I felt compelled to do something. Shastry's daughter is like my own. While we successfully rescued Mira, it unfortunately led to the destruction of the Asura village."

"How long had you known Professor Shastry?" Rohan asked.

"For many years," Hoffmann replied.

Approaching them was a tall, young man with a sleek ponytail, a familiar face that Rohan had seen before.

"Allow me to introduce my friend, Peter Herbert," Hoffmann announced.

Herbert turned towards Rohan, extending a friendly greeting.

"I know you," Rohan stated, his tone laced with anger. "I've seen you before. You were in Berlin, weren't you? You followed Priya and me and were present during Priya's so-called accident. I remember you snatching away my rucksack."

"Please, Mr Sharma," Hoffmann interrupted. "Let me explain."

Ignoring Hoffmann's words, Rohan continued, "You took my rucksack. You stole the Vaimanika Shastra, didn't you? Why would you do such a thing? Amid such a terrible situation, how could you?"

Herbert remained silent, refusing to offer any immediate response.

"And now you come here as if nothing has happened. What do you expect me to say?" Rohan said.

"Allow me to explain, Mr Sharma," Hoffmann insisted. "Peter took the manuscript from you only to protect you. He saved your life and the manuscript."

"So, it was you behind all of this," Rohan said, his agitation growing. "And you call yourself a friend of Professor Shastry?"

"We share a common mission—to preserve these extraordinary ancient manuscripts. They hold great significance for us. If we hadn't taken it from you, there was a risk of it falling into Kali's possession," Hoffmann explained.

"We want to safeguard the manuscript. It is in the best interest of everyone," Hoffmann continued.

"And what do you gain from all of this?"

"We gain freedom. It is our duty to protect ancient knowledge. Preserving our culture and safeguarding our history is of the utmost importance to us."

"You killed Priya to obtain the manuscript, all in the name of saving the world," Rohan cynically remarked.

Herbert spoke, "We did not kill her. I was present during her accident, as you rightly mentioned. I used that opportunity to secure the manuscript, as you also correctly observed. But we did not kill her."

"It was Kali who killed Priya," Hoffmann said. "Kali had intended to target you that day, but luck was on your side. In her attempt to kill you, Priya tragically lost her life."

Rohan's eyebrows furrowed in disbelief. "How can you be so certain?"

"We have been closely observing the activities of the Asuras for a significant period," Hoffmann revealed. "We have extensive knowledge of their movements and intentions. Kali has connections that extend far beyond the boundaries of Lanka. She had been relentlessly searching for the Vaimanika Shastra for many years, aware that the manuscript was in Germany. However, she lacked the precise information until you and Priya stumbled upon it. Didn't you recognise it? Kali and her associates were shadowing your every move."

Rohan pointed at Herbert. "I recognise this man here, but how can I trust your story that Kali was responsible for Priya's death?"

"Herbert can vouch for our claims. He witnessed the tragic events unfold and can shed light on what truly happened."

"Kali orchestrated the sequence of events that led to Priya's death," Herbert said.

The weight of the truth settled upon Rohan, stirring a storm of emotions within. Hoffmann shifted his gaze towards a young woman seated at a nearby table, implying that she held answers to his lingering questions.

Rohan's eyes widened. He recognised her. "Ah, the seer! Uru Aththo. You're Kali's daughter, aren't you?"

The woman nodded earnestly. "Yes, I am. My real name is Abhiravana. What Hoffmann told you is true. My mother ordered her men to kill you, and Priya had to pay the ultimate price. When my mother learnt that you had escaped unharmed, she retreated into hiding."

"Your family seems to have a desire to take lives. So, why did Kali spare my wife, Mira?"

"Do you recall the day we abducted your wife? My mother decided to bring me along. At that time, I lacked the courage to oppose her will. Mira questioned Kali about the reason behind her kidnapping. In response, Kali revealed that it was due to her writing about Ravana.

"Mira spoke words of kindness and understanding about Ravana and Lanka, which softened my mother's heart. Mira promised Kali that she would depict Ravana in a positive light and reshape his image. It was because of this pledge that Kali spared her life. Otherwise, ending her life would have been a simple task for my mother."

"Why do you have the courage to oppose your mother now?"

Abhiravana exhaled softly, her gaze momentarily wandering. "My mother is recovering from her downfall. She has retreated to an undisclosed location, hidden away from the world, even from me. I am tired of continuing the legacy of our ancestors. I no longer desire to spill blood or seek vengeance.

"Retaliation, I believe, yields no true achievements. Instead, I yearn for harmony. I hope my mother can find solace within herself and embrace a different path." Abhiravana's words were proof of her arduous journey to break free from the cycle of violence and seek a new path of peace.

Rohan listened intently to Abhiravana's words. He then turned to Hoffmann and said, "Where's the manuscript now?"

"Let me tell you a story," Hoffmann began, "A group of people came together with a virtuous cause to preserve and protect ancient manuscripts containing powerful knowledge. Their tireless efforts took them to the farthest reaches, unearthing hidden texts from remote corners, forgotten libraries, and concealed tombs across the globe."

Rohan leaned in, captivated by the unfolding narrative.

Hoffmann continued, "Each member brought a distinct skill set, refined through generations of dedicated study and exploration. The group included historians, linguists, cryptographers, and even seasoned adventurers, all united by a profound respect for the ancient wisdom preserved in these texts."

Rohan envisioned the sanctuaries Hoffmann described—fortified vaults and hidden repositories guarding ancient wisdom—and felt a deep awe.

"With great care," Hoffmann continued, "they studied the manuscripts they bought. They believed that the knowledge contained within held immense power and potential, capable of reshaping the world.

"In their pursuit of understanding, the Sangha deciphered ancient languages, unravelled complex codes, and sought to unlock the mysteries hidden in the texts. They understood their responsibility, for their knowledge could shape destinies."

Hoffmann continued, "The Sangha selectively shared portions of the knowledge with trusted people who showed a genuine desire to use it for the betterment of humanity. These chosen individuals became custodians of sacred knowledge.

"While the world remained unaware of the Sangha's existence, whispers and rumours circulated among scholars and intellectuals, fuelling speculation about the hidden guardians of ancient knowledge. Legends told of their involvement in pivotal moments of history, subtly influencing events from the shadows.

"In times of great crisis, the Sangha would emerge, driven by their collective wisdom. They would protect society from those who sought to exploit the manuscripts for personal gain or chaos. Their solemn duty is to ensure the knowledge within the texts would never fall into the wrong hands, carefully balancing the preservation of ancient wisdom with safeguarding our world.

"The Sangha is committed to their mission," Hoffmann concluded.

"When was this Sangha formed?" Rohan's curiosity trickled.

"King Ashoka was the founder. He holds a significant place within the annals of history. Recognising the immense value of ancient manuscripts and their potential to shape society, he became an integral member of the Sangha."

As the conversation delved into the significance of King Ashoka's involvement with the Sangha, Rohan's passion for history began to surface. King Ashoka's reign marked a pivotal moment in India's past due to his military conquests and his subsequent change of heart.

Once a fearsome ruler known for his military conquests, Ashoka underwent a spiritual transformation. After witnessing the devastating consequences of war, he embraced Buddhism and dedicated his life to peace and enlightenment.

With his newfound conviction, Ashoka employed his vast resources and influence to protect and preserve these priceless texts. Realising that knowledge had the power to heal, inspire, and transform, he established specialised learning centres across his empire. Foremost among them were Nalanda University and the University of Taxila.

Nalanda University flourished under the patronage of King Ashoka and became an upholder of knowledge and enlightenment.

"Within its great halls," Hoffmann added, "scholars from various disciplines assembled, studying ancient manuscripts under the watchful eye of the Sangha. Under the guidance and protection of the Sangha, the university became a hub of intellectual exchange, nurturing brilliant minds. The scholars of Taxila were responsible for safekeeping and passing on the wisdom to future generations."

Rohan asked, "You never mentioned the name of the Sangha. Is it called 'The Arya Sangha'? I've heard of it vaguely."

"Rohan, let the confidential group stay undisclosed."

"At least tell me that the Vaimanika Shastra is safe."

"Absolutely safe." Hoffmann nodded.

"I wish I could hold the manuscript in my hands, read it, study it, and gain a deeper understanding of the times of Ravana. Can I borrow it from you for a few days? I promise to give it back to you," he pleaded.

"I understand your curiosity, Rohan, but it's not a wise thing to do. I cannot put your life in danger again. Professor Shastry would have wanted me to ensure its protection as well. The caretakers of ancient knowledge, the Sangha, will take care of the Vaimanika Shastra."

"Why risk your life to protect ancient knowledge that may not even be practically useful?" Rohan asked.

"You are an archaeologist, Rohan. You understand the importance of preserving every fragment of history, of telling the stories of our past to future generations. We must, at all costs, preserve our heritage."

"As Shastry's son-in-law, I owed you this explanation. Now, I think I have repaid Shastry's friendship. Goodbye, Mr Rohan Sharma." Hoffmann and Herbert left.

"What about you, Abhiravana?" Rohan inquired.

"I will be staying here," Abhiravana replied, rising from her seat. "Tomorrow is a very important day, and I wouldn't want to miss it," she added cryptically, walking towards the seashore.

"See you around then," Rohan said, walking towards his room. He changed into his swimming suit to join Mira.

From his room's window, Rohan saw Hoffmann and Herbert walking towards a group of people. He hurried outside to get a closer look, just in time to see a limousine carrying twelve individuals—likely members of the Arya Sangha. Shastry must have been one of them, he thought, but by now, he had probably been replaced by someone new.

Mira indulged in the euphoria of swimming in the vast ocean, finding solace in its rhythmic embrace. It was incredible how the sea brought her the calmness she had longed for. Swimming in the ocean was a unique experience, shaped by the ever-changing nature of the water.

She adapted her movements to the flow, much like the ebb and flow of her own life. The waves guided her breath, leaving little room for choice. Immersed in the water, she found a profound peace and freedom. Far from the land's noise, the blue sea's expanse became her sanctuary, a place where she answered to no one. With each stroke, her mind quieted, sinking into a meditative state and letting go of its fears.

As she returned from the sea and sat on the sandy beach, Rohan joined her, sitting by her side. They shared a quiet moment, appreciating the tranquil beauty of the landscape.

Abhiravana approached them. "There's going to be high tide tonight," she said, her words imbued with a sense of wisdom. "Due to some strange astronomical reasons, the tide will be at its peak at the stroke of midnight, and we will get to see a full moon tonight. We, the Asuras, value the days and months during high tide. I have listened to what my grandmother had to say. I have learnt from her all about the coming of the moon and the flowing of the tides. It's an old prophecy where we believe heaven and earth react for a reason. Would you like to watch the high tide with me?"

"We've had enough adventure for now," he hesitated. "Perhaps it would be best for us to retire to bed."

As the night wore on, weariness gripped Rohan's senses, persuading him to seek solace in bed next to Mira. Nestled together, he found comfort in her reassuring presence.

Yet, sleep eluded him, his mind restless and filled with thoughts. He went to the veranda of their cottage. The ambience outside mirrored the storm brewing within him. Raindrops descended in cascades, adding a touch of melancholy to the night.

Chapter 26
Ravana

> A hundred, bright with fiery flame,
> Fell low before the victor's aim,
> Yet Rávan by no sign betrayed
> That death was near or strength decayed.
>
> —Valmiki Ramayana, Book VI, Canto CIX

In the middle of the night, something made Rohan wake up. His watch showed ten minutes to midnight. He saw Mira deep in sleep. Pulling the blanket on her and spreading it neatly, he left the cottage and walked towards the shore.

The sea appeared restless in the brilliant moonlight, and the scenery was gorgeous. A mellow, milky light from the moon bathed the shore as if the earth, air, and water spirits held their breath for a rare omen. Rohan saw Abhiravana walking on the beach, and he rushed towards her.

"I'm glad you are here." Abhiravana smiled. "Today is special; it only comes once in twelve years." Her uneasiness perpetually grew. "Listen to the sound of the moving water. The moods of nature are very vulnerable. Something strange will happen tonight; I can feel it; my instincts are telling me."

The coastal line appeared empty, with no one except the two of them. "Shush," Abhiravana raised a warning hand. "Listen." At that moment, the moon was upon them, glittering silver swept by like a ghost. She held her ear towards the sea and listened carefully.

Rohan heard no sound except the black water splashing on

the rocks. Abhiravana seemed troubled. She pointed towards a silhouette, walking up from the sea, which was coming towards them, a ghostly figure of a man in a misty outline. It was dark, and there was no other light except from the moon; the man's face was not visible.

There was something about his movement that was different. Rohan knew in his heart that the man in front of them was no ordinary man who might have drowned in water. He saw something else, although he was not sure who or what. As the figure came closer, Rohan caught a first glimpse of the man's haughty eyes.

The sparkle of his eyes in the ghostly grey was like a flash of light in moving water. He could see the spread of his broad shoulders against the moonlight and his long, curly, dark hair, which fell around his shoulders. His figure was accurately defined, and his attire—a dhoti and armour—was visible.

His leather footwear looked old-fashioned and wonderful. He was dark-complexioned and appeared magnificent with his curved features. As Rohan noticed, his mouth frowned under his dark moustache. He drew himself up even more proud and looked at them in the face across the dimness that separated them. The figure now stood only a few feet away.

"He is the mighty Ravana," Abhiravana stated.

With an instinct of curiosity, Rohan followed Abhiravana. Ravana seemed to look at them with the eyes of a living soul. Rohan observed Ravana's strong profile, broad nose, and chin. He also noticed the dark curls of hair cascading over his shoulder, the gold chain around his neck, and the dagger hanging from his belt.

"Who are you?" the figure asked Abhiravana. "You are my descendant, aren't you? I can see the resemblance of your mother." His gesture was graceful, even courtly, and his big fingers were decorated with jewels. The words came out cold and clear.

They communicated in a language Rohan couldn't speak, but somehow, he understood them, although he couldn't fathom how. He stood speechless, staring at Ravana in a horrified paralysis.

"Yes, I am Abhiravana, daughter of Kali." She prostrated to her ancestor.

"So, you are named after me." Ravana lifted his hand in a gesture of blessing, revealing wrists of red velvet. His demeanour was quiet and pensive. The way he raised his hand—strong yet steady, the kind that had once wielded a sword, held reins, scratched words on parchment, and played the Veena—spoke volumes. He must have raised that hand in the past to wage wars, for Rohan was not sure how many.

Ravana wanted to shout but remembered the dignity he owed himself. Then, he turned and looked at Rohan. The glance from the spirit chilled Rohan to the soul. For an instant, his heart seemed to stand still. There was a grim silence within him, but he was not frightened.

Abhiravana introduced Rohan, saying, "Meet Rohan, an archaeologist and a genuinely good person."

Ravana bowed his head like he was greeting. Rohan did the same. A moment later, as they watched, Ravana scooped out the wet sand with his hands and made an idol, a cosmic egg, a Lingam, a symbol of Lord Shiva. He sat in front of it and worshipped the idol by prostrating and chanting mantras like a true devotee of Lord Shiva. The old Sinhala language he spoke was extraordinary, full of epithets and drama. In between his words, the silence of death was upon the night.

Rohan stood like a spectator as if the new world were watching the old millennia-old. There was no sign of life around except for Rohan and Abhiravana. Abhiravana whispered into Rohan's ears.

"Ravana, my ancestor, with a restless soul that has found no peace in the three worlds."

"I have finished my prayers." Ravana stood up. "Perhaps we can converse a little." His voice was clear and cold again, but this time, Rohan noticed a faint tremble as if he were infinitely old and worn. He stood opposite Ravana, looking thoughtfully at Abhiravana, who felt herself shrinking under his gaze.

"I am tired," he said. "The Asuras have become too dangerous. I should not have allowed my family to fight for my respect in society. Imagine, after fighting so hard for my throne, for our freedom, I could not even have a peaceful death. I know, I know, it does not help mourning. I am tired of all the stories that make me a villain, which I am not. I am tired of all the effigies people burn in my name; they even call it winning of good over evil."

He shook his head and moved his dark hair over his bright eyes. He did not move like a living person, and yet again, Rohan had no words to describe what the difference was. There was something beyond human about the gesture that made Rohan's stomach stir.

"Do you know about the modern world?" Abhiravana asked her ancestor.

"Yes." Ravana looked at Abhiravana with amazement. "I know the modern world. It is an honour to be here, vastly different from what it used to be."

"I have avoided the modern way of living—to be like you. I live in the past."

"Oh, the past." Ravana folded his hands. "The past is useful only if you can learn something from it. The present is all that matters. But I am very fond of the past. Come. Let me show you something." He walked towards the shore with a force other than the limbs of his body. They walked inside a cave on a little mountain near the shore.

"Take a light with you." Ravana lifted a burning lamp from the stand nearby and held it up. He moved inside the dark chamber in the cave. Abhiravana took a second lamp, and Rohan followed her.

By the lamp's light, Rohan began to see things—amazing things. He saw an ancient bookshelf, crumbling manuscripts, quills, markers and spikes. A stack of empty parchment and rows of modern volumes were on long shelves.

"This is how I connect with the modern world," Ravana declared.

"A treasure house," remarked Rohan.

A kind of pleasure went over Ravana's face. "It is the result of centuries of collecting. You see, I keep up with the finest modern research. I write my own as well."

Rohan looked around to search for the Vaimanika Shastra.

"You will not find it." Ravana looked at Rohan.

"Pardon me?"

"You will not find the Vaimanika Shastra," Ravana said as if he could read Rohan's mind. "I don't need it any longer."

In one of the corners, Rohan saw an old *Ravanahatha*— an ancient bowed, string musical instrument named after him. Rohan picked it up. "Do you mind if I look at this instrument?"

"Let me show you." Ravana took the instrument from Rohan. "This bow is made of coconut shell and covered with goat skin. A *Dandi*—a bamboo stick attached to this shell, strings made of metal and horsehair. I built this instrument myself," he said proudly.

The longbow had bells attached to it. Holding the instrument in one hand like a violin, he held the bow with his other hand and played the instrument. The melody sounded heavenly. Ravana was no doubt an expert, and he knew the tune he played.

Rohan had heard the melody before, but he was not sure where. He looked at the woodcut of a flying peacock and then turned to Ravana. He was standing before a man who had seen and lived history, a dream come true for the archaeologist in Rohan, who could have never imagined having met such an important historical figure.

"Do you know how to play this instrument?" Ravana looked at Abhiravana, who took the instrument from Ravana's hand and continued playing the same tune Ravana had played before.

"Bravo." Ravana patted her back. "You are my descendant; I am proud of you."

"Why did you bring me here?" Abhiravana's eyes filled with restlessness.

"You are here because you wanted to see me." Ravana's lips twitched with his long moustache.

"What is it that you expect me to do?" Abhiravana questioned his ancestor, "Should I follow in my mother's footsteps, engage in acts of violence and ultimately meet my demise?"

"I have slowly fallen into this bitter lament, searching desperately for Lord Shiva to whom I long to surrender." Ravana paused. "Blows have left scars, but they no longer hurt. Countless nights have passed, and to my surprise, I regret nothing. When I cry, my voice no longer reaches me. I have been waiting long for someone in my family who can change our fate."

Ravana sat magnificently upright in his chair and signalled Abhiravana to sit, but Abhiravana continued to stand. "You will go out into the world," said Ravana, "under my command and write my biography along with my family tree. I will put all my experience at your disposal—good and bad—and you shall bring the power of words."

"Why don't you write this yourself?" Abhiravana suggested.

Ravana smiled. Rohan saw a flash of a different face, as if his dark face had turned white for a second, like that of the dead. "I have other things to deal with now. The world is changing, and I intend to change with it. Soon, I will go to Mount Kailash and never return to Lanka again." He turned, revealing his side profile.

"What is the reason behind your desire to go to the Himalayas? Why do you wish to visit Mount Kailash?" Abhiravana inquired.

"Mount Kailash holds great significance as an ancient and sacred site, older than our current world. It holds cherished memories for me and presents an opportunity to serve my Lord, Shiva, who resides there," Ravana explained.

"Can I go with you? After all, I am your descendant."

"I want you to stay here and take care of these manuscripts and books; it will help you write my memoir. These books hold all that you need to know about your ancestors." Ravana looked at Abhiravana with confidence that might have been fondness on a human face. Then, he stood up with a vigorous, strange movement. "We have conversed enough—I see you both are tired, just like me. Abhiravana, if you wish to talk to me, you know I always listen."

At last, Ravana rose and, without a word, stepped into the darkness so they could no longer make out his form. They walked out of the cave and closed the stone wall behind them. No one could suspect that the mighty Ravana lived inside.

Rohan wondered, turning back and looking at the cave from outside, how Ravana had accustomed himself to this concealed existence and the life of a scholar. He understood the whole thing, Ravana's life, the battles he had fought, hoarse and sweating, in creaking armour, years of baggage he carried on his back like a heavy burden, hoping that it would end one day, in this precise place.

Ravana seemed filled with a profound sense of grief because

he felt the injustice of having to die the way he did. His enemy had pierced him with an arrow, like a wild boar, to kill him. He would have been invincible if his brother had not taken the enemy's side and betrayed him.

Far over the water came the grey light, a sign of a fading night rather than the coming of the morning. The mist was beginning to fade into the water. At that instant, just as Abhiravana was about to touch the Shiva Lingam, there was a loud hiss and murmur of water. A great wave threw over the sand.

The Lingam made of sand was gone, scattered in the sea. Abhiravana sank on the wet sand. Rohan did the same. Then, the waters receded again.

Rohan and Mira headed to the seashore the following day, strolling along the coast. The sky was overcast, but patches of white clouds drifted away as the wind strengthened. Their walk led them to a cliff overlooking a long, narrow inlet. Towering rocks stood together, and they climbed to the top. The summit was bare, marked by a low wall of rock. They sat behind a corner of the wall, offering an unobstructed view of the vast sea. A serene silence enveloped the scene, exuding a sense of calm and optimism.

"Mira, you won't believe what I saw yesterday," Rohan said.

"What did you see?"

"I saw the mighty Ravana."

"In your dream?" Mira teased.

"No, in reality. Last night, I went to the seashore while you were asleep."

"Why didn't you wake me up?"

"I didn't want to disturb your sleep."

"Tell me more. What exactly happened?" Mira's curiosity grew.

"It was unlike anything I've ever experienced before." He paused briefly, collecting his thoughts, and continued, "As the high tide roared and the moon illuminated the night sky, something extraordinary unfolded. I saw Ravana emerge from the depths of the Indian Ocean. It was undeniably him, though he appeared youthful and vibrant, untouched by time. A sense of immense power and profound sadness surrounded him as if he carried the weight of countless years. Ravana, the legendary figure who met his end in a great war, seemed trapped between realms, neither in heaven nor hell. And somehow, I was there to see him."

Rohan reached out, gently grasping Mira's hand. "I know it sounds unrealistic, but I assure you, I was wide awake. Bathed in the moonlight's glow, Ravana rose from the water, and his presence was indescribable. I can't help but wonder what it all means, why Ravana chose that moment, that high tide, to reveal himself to us.

"Abhiravana was with me. Perhaps Ravana's soul seeks release or has a message for the world. All I know is that it was a remarkable encounter that left me with more questions than answers."

"I believe you," she said softly.

"Did he talk to you? Did he say anything?"

"He wants his descendant, Abhiravana, to write his memoir." Abhiravana approached them. "I hope you don't mind if I join you," she said, sitting on a rock nearby.

Rohan nodded. "How are you today?"

"I haven't slept a wink," Abhiravana replied.

"When is your flight?"

"Tonight," Rohan answered.

"My journey has just begun, yet I feel it's coming to an end," Abhiravana said. "I have heard the voice, the voice of Ravana. The secrets of the Asuras have frozen me. Ravana's voice does not allow me to live in peace. The winners take it all. The Devas are the victors here."

"The power of storytelling," Rohan added.

"Rohan, I thank you from the bottom of my heart," Abhiravana said.

"For what?" Rohan inquired.

"I wasn't brave enough to face Ravana alone," Abhiravana confessed. "You accompanied me, and it helped. Meeting Ravana has brought new meaning to my life. I need to understand my purpose. I needed proof that the voice I hear truly belongs to Ravana. Now, I must do something for him, for my family, to reclaim the memories we abandoned long ago."

"Building a new flying machine, perhaps?" Rohan teased.

"No, not at all. We already have too many modern flying machines. I will utilise the ancestral power passed down to me over the centuries. Following Ravana's advice, I will write his biography," Abhiravana said.

"I think it's the right thing to do," Rohan stated.

"I have already begun. I cannot ignore what I hear and feel," Abhiravana said, pausing to gaze towards the sea, rocking herself back and forth. "I am in the hands of fate. There is the voice that speaks, and I cannot ignore it."

"Have you chosen a title for your book?" Mira asked.

"The Asura's Curse—the story of Ravana, the unsung hero," Abhiravana answered.

"I like that title," Rohan commented.

"It's a great start," Mira encouraged.

"After I publish my book, I hope anyone who reads it will

understand that history has two faces. One is the story of the victor often told, and the other is the story of the defeated, rarely spoken of."

"I wish you all the best," Rohan said.

"I hope to see you both again," Abhiravana said as she stood up and left, raising her hand without turning back. Rohan didn't quite understand the meaning behind the gesture, but he felt it wasn't wise to inquire.

Rohan and Mira walked back to the resort. Every now and then, he stumbled on the dunes. His mind swirling with facts and fancies.

That evening, a storm suddenly broke with a flash of lightning that illuminated the entire landscape. A fierce crash of thunder followed swiftly. Soon after, a warm, heavy rain poured down in torrents. As their flight took off, Rohan rested his head on Mira's shoulder and sank into a deep sleep.

Courtesy

Ramayan of Válmíki translated by Ralph T H Griffith [1870-1874]
The Bhagavad Gita, translated by Juan Mascaro [1962]
Staatsbibliothek Berlin/Berlin State Library
Grassi Museum, Leipzig

Acknowledgements

My heartfelt thanks to my literary agent, Mr Suhail Mathur, and his wonderful team at The Book Bakers. It has been a pleasure collaborating with Suhail. His warmth and deep understanding of the publishing world allowed me to focus on my writing, confident that he and his team would expertly handle the complexities of the business. His unwavering support has meant the world to me. I am profoundly grateful for his belief in my work and in me and incredibly thankful for his time and effort in meeting me in Frankfurt.

To Mr Arup Bose and his brilliant team—Ms Stuti Sharma Gupta and Ms Alisha Verma Chopra—at Srishti Publishers & Distributors, I extend my deepest thanks for their guidance and belief in turning my dream of publishing this book into a reality.

To my family, words cannot fully express how thankful I am for the unwavering support of my husband. He has been my first reader, my most honest critic, my inspiration, and my rock through every emotional whirlwind. I am equally grateful to our son for reading the manuscript and providing valuable feedback. Thank you both for joining me on countless journeys, from South Asia to the far reaches of Western Europe and beyond. Your presence and patience have been my greatest gifts.